Homeless Waters

Publisher:
Langaa RPCIG
Langaa Research & Publishing Common Initiative Group
P.O. Box 902 Mankon
Bamenda
North West Region
Cameroon
Langaagrp@gmail.com
www.langaa-rpcig.net

Distributed outside N. America by African Books
Collective
orders@africanbookscollective.com
www.africanbookscollective.com

ISBN: 978-9956-579-51-8

DISCLAIMER

The names, characters, places and incidents in this book are either the product of the author's imagination or are used fictitiously. Accordingly, any resemblance to actual persons, living or dead, events, or locales is entirely one of incredible coincidence.

Homeless Waters

Francis B. Nyamnjoh

Langaa Research & Publishing CIG
Mankon, Bamenda

Contents

Contents

To
Mothering & Teachering

Chapter One

Life in Safang was a well salted and tasty meal. My elder sister and I fought over who would taste the most. Fights aside, we lived our childhood, innocent and pure, with the untamed freedom of the birds of the sky. At least, I would like to believe so. We woke each day with smiles, as Mother strove to please us both. We were happy, maybe because we were still children – virgins to the tossing winds of adulthood. Maybe because Mother was always there, converting our every worry into fantasies of a rosy future. Or maybe because Mother was the only person with whom we lived. Had our father been there as well, it's possible the situation would have been different. We might have sacrificed some of our happiness with a motherly touch for the presence of a father, imposing or not. But we grew up without a father, without even contemplating the necessity of one, and with no knowledge of his whereabouts.

Mother was tall and bubbling with life like a young banana tree growing near a spring. Like the ones down below in the fertile valleys that fed our village and beyond with their bumper harvests. She was kind, gentle, good and simply divine – this, I can still see, as I recollect my childhood, several decades into my adulthood. In fact, I can't remember any cry of mine that went unattended, right from the time when I was a little baby in her arms, up to the age when the first shoots of reason sprouted out and set me wild with thirst for knowing. Harsh words were unknown to her. She greeted everyone with a warm smile. One that sprung from the depths of her heart and reached out – even to those neighbourhood gossips who stuck their noses like antennae into her most personal affairs.

Various young and self confident men came and went. We may not have noticed then why they came and went, but thinking back, I recall that Mother never appeared to have their time. Her determination to reign above trivial and trivialising variants of seduction gained her enormous popularity among the women of her age group. That was significant in neighbourhoods nourished by wild rumours fed by notorious rumour mongers about young beautiful girls ready to elope. Rumours further held that even women, who like Mother already had children, had run away by moonlight at the slightest opportunity to become second or third wives. Marriage, it seemed, was a sought after institution.

But Mother remained steadfast and calm, giving no adventurer room to take advantage. She had learnt to fold and sit upon the risky advice of many who claimed to have her best interest at heart.

Time came and dashed in bundles of happiness, which my sister and I consumed, as we grew, innocent and pure.

When we were about the age to hear and understand the way adults would, Mother told us the story of a man she had loved, our father. It was one evening after an adventurer – one of her most persistent wooers notorious for attending village gatherings only because these were his hunting ground for the wives of others – had babbled and preached and left frustrated, while Mother remained quite unperturbed. We had also eaten and were preparing to retire to bed. That was when Mother, out of some instinct quite unknown to us, decided to talk to us about our father. This was the first time she was mentioning a father to us. So we went and sat next to her by the fireside.

'Your father was not a son of the soil. But he was an admirable man, who believed in the wisdom of his legs.' Mother continued her story, seeing our interest. Not that we in any way had looked forward to this moment, or grown tired of being pointed at as different by the other children who saw themselves as normal and more deserving of the place we called home. We were simply interested in every story Mother told us, being the master storyteller that she was.

'We would be married now if your grandfather had behaved less rigidly. But your grandfather would not hear of any of his daughters getting married to a stranger, a "no man," someone without a base in our land.' She paused, sighed and looked pityingly at us, for the first time ever, to my recollection. I could see she blamed our late grandfather – 'a no nonsense man who knew what he wanted and how he wanted it' – for denying her the right to her first love.

'We thought we could lead father to change his mind by staying together and making children,' she resumed. 'But we were mistaken. Your grandfather warned us that any child we made out of marriage belonged to him and the family. "A child belongs to he who owns the bed," he quoted a famous proverb of the land.'

Mother shook her head as one wounded by the wisdom of the land. Then she turned and faced me directly as if what she would say next was my special concern.

'When he dispatched his final warning to us through a messenger – for your grandfather was too old to travel and we didn't live nearby – I had just conceived you,' she told me. 'Your sister was two years old then. Your father was very offended by my father's intransigence and, instead of staying here to see his children taken away from him, he left in anger to as far off a land as his flexible legs could take him to forget his woe. He has never come back ever since, not even when your grandfather died. It hurts me so much. I miss him terribly – your father. He didn't believe in

3

borders and boundaries, and wanted sons and daughters of all and sundry soils to comingle and intermingle in all freedom.

"'There is wealth in people," your grandfather never tired of repeating. During his days on earth, his ambition had been one: to raise and maintain the largest family in the land, one firmly rooted – a family that would be respected for its numbers even by the royal family. What with all earthly misfortune and providence, he reached his grave too early to attain, but not without untold suffering to his daughters. However, before departing for his grave he left a last word – warning and curse – for any of his daughters who dared to take a stranger back home as husband. Any such daughter was to be ignored by the community of ancestors ever after. He died, hoping his descendants would accomplish what he started and couldn't complete.'

I didn't know what to make of Mother's story, but I felt for her. In my child's mind, my grandfather had no right to an ambition that kept Mother away from the one person who made her happy, and would have made my sister and me normal children.

Two years had elapsed since grandfather died. My sister was now about four years old, though already with the appearance of a seven-year-old. Mother said that Shaka, as my sister was called – which I was later to learn was also the name of a famous Zulu warrior king of old –, had taken after him in kindness, humility and strength of character but resembled our father in hardly any physical way. She was the sort of child the birth of whom would send a suspicious husband sniffing around for evidence that his wife was having an affair. On the other hand, I looked so much like my father and so much unlike Mother that some inquisitive people sometimes went as far as asking if I was really her son. Had she participated actively in my conception? I had heard some curious tongues bleat: had she adopted me?

4

If it was possible for a woman to doubt her baby, she could have doubted I was her son.

I had known neither my grandfather nor my grandmother, who died three years before the birth of my sister. Shaka could at least boast to have been carried by our grandfather before his passing on. The only thing that gave me a distorted idea of what he must have looked like was a portrait photo of him in which his eyes, ears, nose and mouth had all come out double. Mother told us how our grandfather had been so disappointed with the photo, taken with a pinhole camera, that he had refused to pay the cock the photographer had charged for it, and had chased him out of the village, accusing him of witchcraft.

Even though Mother did not stay with him, grandfather always took his granddaughter in his arms whenever he came to Safang on his way to Ndiendie market. When he was about to die, he called Mother and blessed her womb, praying for a baby boy, the root on which the entire family would anchor, so I was made to understand. Boys continue the family line, something that even a girl with a Zulu name like Shaka cannot change. A tradition that must have perplexed my sister beyond words, as in many ways, there was little I could do that she wouldn't do ten times more and a hundred times better.

If grandfather had lived some eight months longer, he would have seen his prayer granted. Mother gave birth to a baby boy and named him Ngoma, after her father. That boy was me.

My sister and I grew up under the exclusive care of Mother. Safang had fertile soil, and Mother was hard working with her hoe. These advantages combined for our survival and for Mother's dignity and resilience.

On market days she made a head load of her produce and took it to Ndiendie to sell to foreigners who came to buy in bulk for resale elsewhere. With the money she bought oil, salt kerosene and other necessities. Then she returned to Safang, bringing some akra balls for Shaka and me. Mother's hard work was largely responsible for our happiness. Every morning she was the first in the village to rise. As early as the second cockcrow, one could hear the sound of her grinding stone turning corn into flour. The sound of the stones in intimate contact reflected her inner joy. If we happened to wake at the sound of grinding, and sometimes her singing as well, she would stop and pat us until we went back to sleep.

Only after all the cooking had been done would Mother wake us. First Shaka, then she would ask Shaka to gently wake her father up.

'Make sure he doesn't get annoyed,' Mother would say. 'Give him first a gentle shake, and don't shout at "father".' She would snap at Shaka whenever she treated me less carefully.

The day was bright by the time we finished eating. Then Mother prepared her basket for the farm. Before setting out she would leave more than enough food for our day's meal. Even though I was big enough to merit less care, Mother never relented asking my sister to take good care of me. If she came back and heard from the child of a neighbour that I had cried during the day, my sister was sure to eat pepper that evening.

Mother loved telling us stories in the evening after all the cooking had been done and we had only to retire to bed. Sometimes she refused telling us any story until we had bathed and were comfortably on our naked bamboo beds. We loved listening to her stories, as we watched the dancing shadows of her evening fire. This she knew, and often she took advantage of it to exercise her disciplinary measures on us.

Mother said certain preliminaries were indispensable if a story had to be told. First, it was a taboo for a child to listen to a story with an unwashed body; that was sure to turn the child mad in later life. Second, no disobedient child could listen to a story and get away unharmed. Thus, it was necessary for any child who wanted a story told to ask forgiveness for all things done wrong, and also to promise obedience. The third and final preliminary was that everybody taking part in storytelling had to learn the words that began and ended every story.

And how her stories were good! We never tired of hearing them. She told her stories with honey on her tongue. Lowering or raising her voice, she brought on fear, joy, triumph or sadness at just the right moments. We lived the worlds and experiences of her stories. Those were times when happiness laced every activity like rain showers at the heart of the rainy season.

Life in Safang was well seasoned. We played about with other children our age and learnt to shun boredom. On non farm days, Mother took us to her kin in nearby villages. There was our grand-uncle who lived in Ngunakhan. He was a good hunter in his capable days, and as an old man had passed his gun, spears, nets and dogs to his eldest son and retired, 'to spend the rest of his days like a woman' he would say, telling stories to everyone with idle ears. Even then he found it difficult to be still, so he took his knife and went back to his raffia bush, which he had abandoned in his more active days. He was a man capable of many things good. His wine was particularly sweet and tasty, especially when mixed with corn flour porridge. We always asked Mother to take us to him when she could. He was funny and would tell us with a face of total disappointment, at least, so it seemed to me, how he had died several times without success, as each time his ancestors saw him coming, they would chase him back saying, 'What's your business dying? Death is not for you!' We never stopped laughing when we were with him.

'Good day "brother",' he would greet me.

'Good day grand-uncle,' I would say.

'I am your brother and not your grand-uncle. So never make the mistake of calling me grand-uncle again.' My grand-uncle never ceased telling me this.

I can't say how many times I had promised not to call him grand-uncle. But whenever I found myself standing in front of him, I didn't understand why he should cease to be grand-uncle.

'I hope your daughter has not denied you food,' continued my grand-uncle. 'I hear it said these days that the aged are too useless to deserve food. And I wonder whether those who say this have forgotten there was a time they themselves could have been considered too young to be fed.'

We all laughed, more at how he said what he said than at what he said. Then he would call me and offer me a seat and a horn-cup, saying: 'Drink this wine with me. It is only for those too old to eat.'

I always made to give my sister some, but my grand-uncle would not permit Shaka, older though she was, to drink directly from my horn-cup.

'Ask her to bring a little clay pot if you are so bent on giving her some of our wine.' My grand-uncle would pause and gulp the wine as if it had suddenly improved immensely in quality.

'Are these not the very women who say we are too old to eat? Or are you not aware of the fact that you are old?' he would ask looking at me.

According to my grand-uncle I was more of my grandfather than just in name. He firmly considered and believed me to be his brother Ngoma, for which reason I had to take up my grandfather's responsibilities and enjoy all privileges he used to enjoy. It was for this reason that my grand-uncle treated me the way he did. But to Shaka and me, he was only being funny. We were too small to understand.

When we had been long with him and were about to
return home, my grand-uncle would call me into his bedroom
and share with me 'words of wisdom'. Then we would both
come out and shake hands in the eyes of everyone. Finally
he would ask me to take care of my daughter and
granddaughter.

'Make sure you give them enough to eat and to do,
"brother". Take care of them. Beware of the Njangmans…'
He always warned me against the Njangmans – which only
much later I came to understand referred to the Germans –
even though there were no Germans left. Because, as he
would put it, 'The Njangmans, while withdrawing during
the world war, tried to steal the Sacred Spitting Stone on
the way to the palace, but the stone kept escaping back to
its original location. And when they tried to set the palace
on fire, the palace would not burn…' To him, the Njangmans
were people to be watched at close range, and I had the
duty of protecting Mother and Shaka from them, whom he
was sure were still around.

Once out on the road back home, Shaka and I would
laugh. I could imagine the Sacred Spitting Stone running
for its dear life, on magical legs as the Njangmans chased
with guns, spears and machetes. Mother just smiled at the
old man. I tried to understand why I should be counted
among those too old to eat, and why my grand-uncle kept
urging me to take care of Mother and Shaka with statements
such as, 'The wishes of children are like the wishes of kings.'

Our compound was like the ear of Safang village. It was
the first compound on the way from Ndiendie, or the last
through which traders passed on their way to Ndiendie
market, which was held twice a week. My sister and I, as
well as many other children in the neighbourhood, were used
to the movements of traders to and from the market up in
the hills. On market days we hung about the road with other
children looking expectantly at every passerby. Sometimes,

kind ones among them gave us sweets, biscuits and big loaves of soft bread. The tradition among us children was to divide equally amongst us anything that happened to fall our way.

On one such market day a passing trader gave a small loaf of soft bread to the boy who was standing closest to me. Instead of behaving traditionally, this boy immediately threw the loaf into his mouth expanding like that of a python and snapped it shut to chew. Our furious lot fell on him and tore his mouth open, bringing out bits of smashed bread smeared with greedy saliva. Our shouts had brought our parents to their doors. As I forced into my mouth the bits of bread I had snatched out of the greedy victim's mouth, Mother caught sight of me. For the first time ever she called me by name.

'Ngoma, what is this?' She was furious. 'Stand there! Don't run.' And she ran down from the door where she had stood. She seized me in her hands and forced the bread out of my mouth.

'I've told you not to bring disgrace to your mother. How many times have I sung to you to ask me if you need anything?'

As she spoke, she shook me until my head spun round and my eyes seemed as if they were coming off. Then she carried me to the house where she gave me money to buy a loaf for myself. Nothing could be sweeter than Mother's love.

The very day Mother forced the bread out of my mouth, a trader strayed into our house and asked to be housed for the night. He told Mother his market had been so good that it blinded him from realising how dark it had grown until the last customer had left him.

'It is not always that one has a good market day,' the man explained to Mother. 'And when a day like today comes, it blocks one's consciousness to passing time. Today was really my day. I had cargo amounting to ten head loads, but not up to one head load is left unsold!'

The trader was very pleased with the way things had turned out for him that day. Mother was studying him critically. When she had built up her impressions she spoke to the trader.

'Here we are friendly to everybody. We try to look at things with the eyes of others. How else can we fathom what it means to see like another person? We are happy to receive you. We welcome you.'

On hearing this, the trader thanked Mother wholeheartedly.

Mother asked Shaka to give the trader some water. He washed his hands and ate the fufucorn and vegetable that Mother had placed before him. Then he thanked Mother once more.

'You could use that bed,' Mother told the trader as she pointed at a bed across the room. 'My children and I can use this one on which I am sitting.'

Mother heated up some water with which the trader bathed. Then he went to bed and covered himself with the new blanket Mother had bought two markets ago.

The following day, before setting out on his way home, the trader gave Shaka two sets of earrings.

Mother declined one of them saying, 'She has got only two ears, how many earrings can she wear?'

Shaka showed no displeasure at being reduced to a single set of earrings, when until then she had worn little more than bits of broom to keep the ear piercings open.

The trader gave Mother some money and promised to pass again. At first Mother hesitated. She would not have his money. But the trader explained that it was not a payment for her invaluable hospitality, just a modest sign of gratitude. Put that way Mother found it difficult to refuse his money.

The trader passed again as he had promised, not once, not twice, but every time he attended the Ndiendie market, which was twice every week. Thus the trader was sure to stop by our house four times in the week, twice when going up to and twice when coming down from the market. Each time he came he brought Mother and us various gifts. We gradually grew used to him, partly because we no longer stood by the road to wait for gifts, and partly because he was also a good storyteller. His friendship with Mother grew daily, rising like dry garri soaked in cold water. Mother created a special menu every market day to please him, from which Shaka and I indirectly benefitted.

With time the neighbours learned and approved of Mother's friendship with the trader whom we now called Lumawut. Mother had introduced Lumawut to our grand-uncle. The first thing she did was to bring along some tobacco which our grand-uncle had refused saying:

'I like tobacco quite alright. But it is not from everyone that this tobacco should come. I don't know this trader of yours. Why then should I be anxious to know only his gift of tobacco. That, I think is putting my hand into a deep dark hole.'

Mother heard and understood. When Lumawut came next, she asked him to stay for an extra day so they could go and see her uncle together. He blamed her for surprising him, but he still looked into his market things for a gift. He found a raincoat and decided upon it.

Our grand-uncle's impressions were positive. Lumawut was a man of medium height and a strong build. He looked firm and responsible and our grand-uncle was happy. He appreciated his raincoat and his tobacco, which as Lumawut said were just the heralds of many future gifts.

Everybody other than those men who had tried and failed was in favour of Mother's friendship with Lumawut. He now intermingled with the local people of the village, particularly the men. He even joined the community development group made up of young men of Safang. And though he was seldom present during its working sessions, he always sent some money for food and palm-wine for the regular others. The only time he had ever been present was when this group of young men had to clear Mother's farm. That day, people went home more pleased than ever with what they had eaten and drunk. Lumawut soon became the most popular man in Safang. He seemed to have learnt in his youth how to please.

Mother and Lumawut were friends now for a whole year, without a single quarrel or misunderstanding between them. They approached each other with mutual respect, understanding, and the fear of provoking the unknown, or so it seemed to my baby senses.

One day, when Lumawut had come and gone as usual, Mother called Shaka and me, and told us that in two weeks we would be living with Lumawut in his village.

'Where is this village of his, Mother?' Shaka asked.

'Far down below the mountains on a plain called Bonfuma, where they say our people are most civilised. It is very far away from here,' Mother took the pains to explain.

'Why must we go and live there with him, Mother?' I asked.

'You see, father, I need support. As you two grow, so do I realise the need for support. Not just any type of support, but support from a man.' She looked far away deep in thought.

'But can't he come and live with us here? Must we go to him, Mother?' Shaka asked.

'It is difficult for you to understand, Shaka. But we can't do otherwise. We just have to go and live with him.' Mother paused and seemed to feel a new and apparently more convincing reply open up in her mind. Then she continued, 'Moreover, Lumawut is a trader, and most of what he has to sell is only available that way. It is more convenient for him to remain there.'

13

'If we leave this place, Mother,' I was asking, 'don't you think that when he comes to sell his things he will have no place to stay? Who will eat the sweets, biscuits and soft bread he is going to bring? They will get bad, don't you see that?'

Mother was infinitely patient. She avoided leading me to feel that my questions were ridiculous.

'Father, don't you think that now he has become an active man in this village, he can hardly lack a place to stay? Even if no one else would, my uncle would readily house him. So there is no problem there. As regards your gifts, instead of bringing your sweets, biscuits and soft bread here, he will carry them to Bonfuma where you can always have them in abundance. Don't worry, father. Don't think you will miss anything. Rather, the way will be open for many more new things. It will be just like home away from home, only much more exciting.'

Yes, we loved to see new things more and more, both my sister and I. We were anxious to go to that part of our vast country where the people were said to be 'the most civilised of us all.' I wanted to be more civilised – to eat and drink and breathe Civilisation. My sister wanted Civilisation too. So we were both happy to follow Mother to Bonfuma, Lumawut's faraway fountain of exciting new things to come. Our growing curiosity to discover and embrace the unknown made the two weeks seem as long as two cumbersome years. I began counting the days as they came and passed into nights, but soon I lost count. I think I even lost grip of what two weeks meant in time. When I asked Mother she explained to me that when four Ndiendie market days have come and gone, two weeks would have passed. But it was a long time, particularly as Lumawut was not going to come and sell at the market. He would be preparing to come and take us down to Bonfuma.

The time came at long last. Lumawut came with three solid men and two women of middle age, all his relations. Two of the young men carried a tin of oil each, while the third carried a bag of salt. The women carried huge baskets full of corn flour, and Lumawut himself carried two big cocks – a red and white one – in a giant perforated bamboo basket, a *kquem*.

Lumawut and his people put down their loads and came into the house for a little rest. Mother had prepared a very special meal of fufucorn and vegetable soup full of egusi. They ate and drank the palm-wine that Mother had bought from our grand-uncle that morning. Lumawut detailed her on certain things to be done and set out with his people to Ngunakhan, where the whole ceremony would be carried out at our grand-uncle's place. Everything had to proceed as custom would have it, for a marriage to be valid in the eyes of the community.

Chapter Two

Bonfuma is a vast plain bounded by two rivers with a long history. People coming there from Ngong-Ngong and beyond have to cross the Ngong River that flows along the boundary. The other river runs along the eastern boundary between Bonfuma and Song-Kang village and takes its name from the latter. This Song-Kang River, we crossed last the day we were coming from Safang. Indeed, I remember that evening particularly well, and I still think of the terrible fear that seized me at the sight of the long, narrow, fragile bridge of delicately woven rope that linked our end of the river to the brother end that stood on Bonfuma soil. I recall Mother confessing to Lumawut and his men that that was her first time seeing such a long and shaky bridge over a river hungry for those who dared to put a foot wrong. So the strongest of Lumawut's men carried Mother across, while one of the women took Shaka on her back as Lumawut himself crossed the bridge with me sitting across his shoulders. This memory sticks to my mind as chewing gum to one's hair.

Both rivers are broad, deep and usually gentle, and their fertile banks attract farmers. But when it rains and they welcome the homeless waters chased from the hills, they become wildly intoxicated and flooded nearby farms and carried away crops, leaving behind alluvial promise of widespread starvation. These rivers are as harmful as they are useful. Fishermen with hooks and nets can be seen exploring their banks and depths when the waters subside a little after a few days' sunshine, or when the volumes are completely low in the dry season. Also in the dry season,

17

those interested in sand can gather huge amounts of it along the river banks to build or make money. After a devastating flood, women can be seen in their various riverside farms and along the banks of the two rivers fetching firewood.

Lumawut's compound was nearer the Ngong River than the Song-Kang River, but it was remarkably far from both. This distance did not deter him from acquiring farmland along the banks of the two rivers. Unlike many of his peers, he was not the sort of man to let an opportunity pass. In Bonfuma, staying close to fertile farmland was not an automatic advantage when it came to owning land. Proof of this was the uneasy fact that big men as far away as Ngong-Ngong village had farms right in Bonfuma. Land in Bonfuma village belonged to the powerful, not in terms of physical strength but in the sense of those who mattered. As was the way with power, a lazy man's claim to a piece of land passed down to him by a hardworking father was even more temporary if the man in question did not matter much in the affairs of the village. Hard work alone did not guarantee to land ownership, but it was already a good sign for a village that was simply too populated to be interested in people who let grass flourish uninterruptedly.

Lumawut's compound comprised a big house with an aluminium roof and two one-room thatched houses, one of which seemed to have been newly constructed. The whole compound was surrounded by flourishing banana and plantain trees as well as a few trees I could not name, and a handful of coffee plants. The banana and plantain trees were so close together and so unkempt that it was practically impossible for anyone outside the compound to make out even the roofs of the three houses. Unless the sun was standing overhead, it went unobserved in his compound. But for the short time when the sun stood overhead, we in that compound were shielded from view as shadows shifted with the sun. We ran out of the enclosure every now and then to know what position of the sky the sun had attained. We hardly felt the inconvenience of the overbearing trees, although we may very much have loved an unfiltered version of the Civilisation we had come to embrace.

We had already been in this compound for a year – a year full of incidents, a year of blissful experiences for me in particular. I was a pupil of the only primary school in the whole of Bonfuma and the nearby villages. And Lumawut had told me more than once that the teacher had confided in him that I was doing well. As a sign of his appreciation for my being a hardworking pupil, he started calling me 'My Teacher', whenever he spoke to others about me. There was pride in him when he used this name, not having himself been to school. As if to make the point that everyone has something to teach everyone, he took time and pains to teach me how to ride his bicycle, one of only ten in the entire village. I was proud of him, very proud of him.

My sister Shaka did not go to school with me. It wasn't the tradition to send women to such places, since they would soon marry and join a new household. All money spent on them would be gone for nothing. No, it was no good sending girls to school. That is how the argument went, and that was the rationale for Shaka's stay at home. With eyes watered by tears of pain and envy she watched me go and come from Monday to Friday. I felt bad for her, and would share with her some of the new songs I learnt – songs about distant places and distant things on mysterious themes, that we were compelled to sing by teachers who knew best what was good for us. Of all the songs I learnt and shared with Shaka, her favourite was: '1, 2, 3, 4, 5. Can you catch a fish alive? Why did you let it go? Because it bit my finger so. 6, 7, 8, 9, 10…' It was in this way she came to master numbers and avoid being cheated on market days, when she accompanied Mother to sell the food items they harvested with long distance traders in mind.

In her element, Mother had worked in three of Lumawut's farms already and planted maize, beans, groundnuts and vegetables. The rivers had made the Bonfuma soil very fertile by their constant flooding during the heavy rains. All the alluvial soil they washed away from farms uphill and along their courses was deposited on farms in the Bonfuma plain. Here the crops looked rich and healthy, and took a relatively short time to attain maturity. People up in the Safang hills always received, with curious surprise, news that maize had already been harvested in Bonfuma, at a time when not even the fastest and earliest farmer could boast of maize the size of a swollen armpit. There was also a fourth farm where sugarcane grew. It had been planted by Lumawut's first wife. All Mother did on the sugarcane farm was weed it and plant a few more plants.

Whether Lumawut had let Mother know that he was already married and she was coming to Bonfuma as a second wife, I can't say, but I doubt very much he did. Whether he did or did not, one thing is certain. We arrived at his compound to see a woman – his first wife. She was wrapped in a thick cloth of anger when she saw us. She just sat in her one-room house and welcomed none of us, not even her husband. As she stared at us with indignation, I could see she was crying. She refused to answer when her husband greeted her. She remained seated like a piece of wood. Only her daughters came to receive their father and us. Maybe they welcomed us because they didn't understand what our coming meant. They played around Mother after eating what she had offered them, the remains of our journey's delicious snacks. They were innocent little children, very much like Shaka and I.

Lumawut asked Mother to assume temporary usage of the newly constructed one-room house while waiting for a bigger one to be built. Our things were squeezed in and that night passed. The following morning, a little before dawn, we were awakened by a quarrel. The voices were quite distinct and we had no problem hearing what Lumawut and his first wife were quarrelling about.

'I've told you I can't share this compound with another woman. You either take her back to where you got her or I will take myself away!' The first wife was shouting at the top of her voice as if what she was saying was not intended just for her husband's ears.

'I cannot send her away and I don't want to lose you.' Lumawut's voice was low.

Mother who had been lying on the bed on her back became alert and took up her head which she supported with her left hand. She listened to the first wife who had started threatening again.

'I've said my mind. You lose your new love or I leave – this morning! I don't want any more fooling. Now I understand all the trading up in the mountains. You stayed away for weeks saying marketing was adverse. Now I understand this new house you quickly built. You said it was for my sugarcane. I've had enough. You take her back or I step out – with my children!' Her fury rose like a storm – ready to blow roofs off his buildings and carry away.

'Go alone if you must. Leave my daughters out of it.' Lumawut's voice was calm and steady.

'I'll go with them! You've paid nothing to my parents, so the children belong to them!'

She dashed out of his house into hers, where her daughters were still enjoying a calm sleep. She woke them up and turning a deaf ear to their questions, began assembling her belongings. Her daughters blindly joined her, still unsteady with unfinished sleep. Every single thing of hers was packed. She finished before sunrise, because her things were not many. Then she left Lumawut's compound with her two daughters. They were weeping, all three of them.

21

Weeks gave way to months which disappeared into years, but Lumawut remained calm. He refused to do what every other man would have done even within the first few days of his first wife's departure. He failed to go and plead in front of her and her parents. It may be that Mother had already captured his heart entirely. Or perhaps his heart was beyond capture. Or maybe there was no heart to capture. It pains me so much even now remembering how the woman and her daughters left Lumawut's compound weeping bitterly.

* * *

I still remember very well the first day I went to school. It was Lumawut himself who took me there. He held my little left hand, and we walked the half mile that linked our compound and the school. That particular day must have been set aside for the admission of new first year pupils. When I looked around I saw boys who like me were accompanied by someone bigger or those who were big enough to forego a guide, but all of whom looked as strange to the place as I was.

The Headmaster of the school knew Lumawut by name. He greeted him and walked up to where we were standing. 'Is this the boy you talked of the other day?' the Headmaster asked, hitting his left hand with the pen he held loosely in his right hand.

'Yes, he is the son I told you of,' Lumawut answered respectfully.

'Don't you think he is too small?' The headmaster asked as he placed the hand with the pen on my head. Giving Lumawut no time to tell him it was very necessary I go to school that year, he said, 'Don't worry very much Mr. Lumawut. We are going to learn the truth about him in a very practical way.'

As he spoke he took my right hand and, passing it over my head, tried to make it touch the bottom of my left ear. But all his efforts were in vain.

'There is just no hope for him this year,' said the Headmaster shaking his head. 'In a village like this where ages cannot be determined precisely, the best and most practical way to see if a child is the right age for school is to pass his hand over his head and see if it can touch his ear on the other side. And your son's hand is far from the target, Mr. Lumawut. This clearly shows that he is still unripe for formal learning. Try him again next year.'

Lumawut pleaded at length, but the headmaster seemed to have sealed his mind for good. Just when he was about to give up and return home to wait for next year, a new idea struck Lumawut in the head.

'Oh! You see! Too much talking would have made me forget to tell you that the scarce cloth you asked me to look for has been found at last, though not in great quantity. I have decided not to tamper with it until you have got the required quantity for your wife.' When he had said this he had the impression things might take a favourable turn.

'Well done. I hope you will give it to me at a special price.' And he looked at Lumawut directly in the face.

'It is a very expensive cloth. You know that very well. But I am not going to get rich by using good friends like yourself,' replied Lumawut, his face oiled by a broad smile. 'Just come to the house in the evening and we will fix it. I can even give a fathom to you at the very price which I bought it. It is not today that we are friends.'

The Headmaster was happy as could be read from his face that shone with knowledge and knowing. Lumawut held my hand and made as if he was going. The Headmaster stopped him with a question.

'Mr. Lumawut, are you too impatient to get your son admitted this year? Can't you just wait till next year when he will be the right age?' His voice was a mixture of tender confusion, impatient with feeling compelled to concede.

Lumawut cleared his throat and said, 'I would have waited if I were the only one behind his going to school this year. But the Mother is even keener than I. She has just come in and I haven't yet learnt to fall out with her. She is the crux of the problem.' He spoke like someone with his hands tied behind his back.

'Now, Mr. Lumawut, understand this. His admission is strictly conditional. Any truancy or underperformance will lead to him being sent out again. You must agree to these terms before I can do anything.'

Lumawut did not even hesitate. 'I am in perfect accordance,' he said.

'Then bring him to my office right away. What name do you want him to bear?'

'Ngoma Lumawut.' The answer was so automatic that I had the impression it had been ready in his mind for the past two days, ever since he began discussing with Mother about sending me to school.

That is how I became a pupil of the Bonfuma Mimboland Baptist Mission School, and the day after the admission Lumawut handed me to a big boy he knew well to take care of me in school. The school compound was vast and full of big houses with aluminium sheet roofs. These houses were partitioned into large classrooms where various pupils sat on wooden benches under the supervision of a class teacher. There was also an orchard with an extensive variety of fruit trees. And there was a big field where pupils went to play during breaks.

That first day at school, nothing serious was done. After a preliminary cleaning up of the classrooms, the bell rang for classes to begin. We were introduced to our class teacher, a short man with a large pot belly that made him look like a woman in the last months of pregnancy. He loved sitting on the table instead of using the stool meant for him to sit behind his table. He told us a few things which he promised to deal with the following week, it being a Friday and the end of the school week. He also made each and every one of us promise to bring along on Monday smooth banana leaves and a sharpened piece of bamboo with which to write in class. Then he promised twenty lashes for anyone who forgot to come to school with twenty counting sticks daily.

It is only after we had assured him that these materials would be ready for use on Monday morning that he relaxed his heavy belly and began a seemingly interminable session of storytelling. All his stories came from the Old Testament of the Bible. He had told them for such a long time that he hardly looked at the Bible that lay open beside him. The stories he told were so good that the morning period passed unnoticed.

When the bell rang the big boy entrusted with taking care of me came from Class Five A to fetch me in Class One C.

'What is the bell for?' I asked him.

'That we should go and eat,' the boy answered.

'Where are they giving the food?' I asked.

The boy laughed and explained that every pupil was to eat what he had carried from home. He said he had brought no food for us because our compound was nearby and we could rush home and eat and make it back in time for afternoon classes. I felt like spitting in his face, for how could one rush home and eat and rush back without expending all the food one had eaten? It was like satisfying hunger only to be hungry again. So I resolved there and then never again to come to school without food.

That was my first day in school. As the term flew on, Lumawut constantly reassured me that I was not doing badly. It was the short, fat-bellied teacher who confided in him whenever they met in a drinking house or elsewhere.

25

Still, at first I found it difficult. It took me a considerably long time to become used to school life. My initial difficulty might have been largely caused by my careless and light-hearted attitude towards learning, though the unserious personality of my teacher who always avoided using his stool might also have played a part. This dangerous attitude of mine would have continued if not for Mabuh, the big boy under whose care Lumawut left me. His promptness in fetching me for school each day and his strictness at school gradually pushed me to be more serious. As time passed and as the teacher gave more and more corporal punishment, my interest in school grew, and not only because I nursed a fear for the teacher's painful cane. The growth in interest could also be attributed to the fact that deep inside me, I wanted to do everything not to give the Headmaster cause to realise his admission-day threat to send me home for underperforming.

Eventually, my school life flowed uninterruptedly like huge logs of firewood down a flooded plain by Ngoma, a river named after my great grandfather, a name passed down to me in his honour.

Mother, besides being a naturally very hardworking woman, had passed almost all of her early adulthood on her own without her father and had learned to work independently. She rarely went to somebody to ask for help with any problem she could solve herself. She accomplished her farm work almost entirely on her own, even things for which women would instinctively turn to men for assistance. The soil in Bonfuma was softer than the soil in Safang, and she needed none of Lumawut's manly help to do the preliminary clearing and digging. Within the first two years of her stay in Bonfuma, Mother produced so much corn that Lumawut was forced to build the fourth house earlier than he might have planned. He built a two-room house like that in which he himself lived. Mother's hard work and initiative in domestic matters pleased Lumawut very much, leaving him with little cause to quarrel.

With some of the abundant corn she harvested twice a year, Mother made *kang*, an alcoholic drink which she sold on market days. Within two years she had joined the women's weekly savings society, and she became one of the highest savers. Allowed, she would have joined even the men's society and out-saved quite a few of its members. But that would have been seen by the men as an affront. It was a serious taboo for a woman to openly equate herself with any man, no matter how abominably low his social status. She could do so in private, but never in public. Having started life with Mother doubling up masterfully as mother and father, I thought it terribly unjust for men to seek to dwarf women.

Our junior was delivered in the second month of our third year in Bonfuma. Lumawut who had waited for a frustratingly long time was overjoyed when Mother first broke the news that she had conceived a baby. He was tender towards her and his care for her increased as his daily hopes mounted that the baby could turn out to be a boy.

When the baby turned out to be a girl instead, I could clearly see disappointment like a wooden carving on Lumawut's face. His mountains of hope had been shattered and carried away by the rivers of reality. He moved about like one forced to work by the devilish forces of evil, performing the necessary rites in complete dejection. Lumawut was one of those men who seemed to have been reared in one of those family backgrounds where the disparity between men and women was overly dramatised. He just failed to see anything useful in girls beyond their subjection in domestic duties. His first two children were girls, and he had worked and hoped for a difference with Mother.

Mother read the disappointment in Lumawut's face and was sad. She felt his piercing eyes glare accusingly. Did he sincerely believe she had gone shopping for a girl? If a boy

27

had been there in her womb she would surely have given birth to him. You can't plant a mango and expect to harvest an avocado can you? How could Lumawut have given her a girl only to turn around asking for a boy? What caprice was that?

His moodiness continued for a long time and Mother could not bear it. She was very unhappy and refused to eat most of the time. This must have affected the baby too for it soon began to reject the milk Mother tried to make it suck from her overflowing breasts. The situation would have continued, and with fatal results perhaps, had not a wise and trusted friend of Lumawut's come to speak to him upon noticing the drama that was playing out.

'You must understand. God knows what he does. Do not be angry lest he notes that you are trying to contest the way he distributes his children. Do not endanger your life and that of innocent children and their mother. Have you no eyes to see that your strange disposition is tearing your wife into pieces and making the child grow thin with hunger?'

The friend was speaking to Lumawut in the latter's house, where they were sitting alone behind closed doors, though what they said was within my earshot, since I was listening keenly by the door. Lumawut brought his friend palm-wine but the friend kept it aside saying it could be attended to after more important matters had been settled. Little wonder that this friend of Lumawut was called Wutaseba – "the person who sees what those blinded by sight can't"!

Lumawut was not all that convinced that his behaviour was responsible for the adverse change in Mother and my little sister. So he argued, 'My disappointment is a personal one. I've pointed no accusing finger at my wife. I've not even mentioned to her that I am disappointed. So I don't see why there should be a correlation between my internally borne grief and physical changes in my wife and daughter.' Convinced he had made a clincher argument, he threw open his hands to emphasize his disbelief.

'Don't be a fool, Lumawut,' his friend said. 'Do you want to tell me that people can only act on what you say and not what you do? Your eyes clearly show what you think about your daughter. Your disgust for her has covered every bit of fatherly love. Your eyes are also guilty of wrongly trying to accuse your innocent wife, and your entire body speaks a language of its own in this matter. Take your time and save yourself from the heavy hammer of divine justice that strikes down fools and those who dare too far. Beware that God doesn't act before you change.' With these words Wutaseba opened the door and, expressing no surprise at seeing me, walked briskly across the compound to Mother's two-room house. He greeted her, carried the baby for some time and left the compound with his blessings and wisdom.

From that day, the abnormal Lumawut brusquely resumed his usual self again. He once more became tender with Mother and softened his glares towards the baby. Mother felt the change and quickly recovered. Surprisingly too (or unsurprisingly perhaps) a few days after Mother's recovery my little sister turned back to the breast she had rejected. In two weeks she completely regained her health, bloom, and bubbly disposition.

Apart from such moments of tension and gloom that sprang from one misunderstanding or another between Lumawut and Mother, life for the first seven years in Bonfuma was in many ways just as Mother had predicted, home away from home.

Chapter Three

By the end of the seventh year in primary school, I had written two major examinations whose importance could hardly be overstated. One of them, the Common Entrance, qualified the successful pupils for Secondary grammar schools, while the other, the First School Leaving Certificate examination, left an indelible stamp of achievement on the foreheads of the successful, as its absence carried the unsuccessful and unfortunate pupils into the land of eternal oblivion.

I had worked hard for both examinations. It wasn't easy writing them, let alone passing them. One needed a lot of willpower and patience. It was like going hunting or onto a battlefield. There is no point if you have not prepared yourself or your weapons. One also needed to travel, since examinations were taken in Lakbih. Lakibih was a faraway place with people who spoke a tongue strange to ours. It was more than forty miles away from Bonfuma and needed a whole day's trekking for the very youthful and energetic in our village. Whenever there was an examination to write in Lakibih, those concerned would leave Bonfuma two days before to give themselves enough time to rest and revise. Bonfuma was too small a village to form an examination centre of its own. All its class seven pupils wrote both major examinations in Lakibih where there was a government school ten times bigger than the former Mimboland Baptist Mission School that had – to our greatest joy at being able to study free of charge – been taken over by the government two years before I wrote my final examinations and become known as Government School Bonfuma. The travel made it doubly painful and discouraging to fail either or both of these examinations. Failure entailed another year of donkey work and, a year later, yet another forty mile trek.

I passed the Common Entrance Examination in list A, which made me eligible for a free education in a government college. The nearest government college at the time was hundreds of miles away in an unknown land called Mbengom. My class seven teacher, the very caring, understanding and inspirational Mr. Samson Samba, a well informed man of Bolingfomfom origin, advised me to choose that college. He brought the good news of my excellent exam performance right to Lumawut's compound and asked me to prepare for my interview. But Mr. Samba and I arrived in Mbengom a week too late for the stipulated interview. The Principal refused to listen to what he considered our audacious complaint that there was not a single radio in the whole of our village. He provocatively asked my teacher what he was doing with all the money he took as a salary that he couldn't buy a radio. Mr. Samba ignored him, and we returned home with bad news for Mother and Lumawut.

However, to please Mother who had given a timely birth to a baby boy Lumawut had proudly named after his late father, he took me to a college at a cold hilly place a hundred and fifty miles away called Nsong, famous for its kola nuts and for being the first in the region to embrace the white man of God wholeheartedly. This college belonged to the Catholic Church and was named after St. Martin. The Principal, Reverend Father Michael Blackwater – a tall, imposing presence with a face almost entirely dominated by a long thick beard – looked for my Common Entrance Examination results in the booklet of successful pupils that he kept handy on his office table and expressed great satisfaction. He asked me to read a passage from a book on the Holy Ghost Fathers and their good work in West Africa,

32

which I believe I read well, except for some of the names which were difficult to pronounce. Then he gave me a very brief interview.

'Are you a Catholic?' he asked in his unclear white voice.

'Yes, Sir,' I answered with respect.

'Say "Yes, Father", and not "Yes, Sir." Do you hear me?'

'Yes, Father,' I said timidly.

'You surely are not a Christian. Are you?'

I didn't understand what he meant exactly, but I responded what I was sure about.

'I am a Catholic Church member, Father.'

He smiled and said, 'I meant whether you are baptised?'

'Not yet, Father.'

'Do you promise to enrol for baptismal doctrine as soon as you set foot in this college?' he asked, looking up at Lumawut who, unable to understand a word of English well spoken, looked down at me for interpretation.

I immediately spoke out to the Father. 'I do promise, Father.' And seeing that he was still unsatisfied, I added, 'My father wanted me to give my name for Catechism in our local church. Only he decided it was better for me to do it after my examinations. He is himself a strong Christian baptised by Father Anthony of Momlong.' I was very lucky that the Father did not distrust me. If he had but suspected and referred to the list of Father Anthony's Christians in the copy of the church logbook in his keeping, he would have been utterly shocked, and I would have been in a great mess. I thanked my stars that he didn't bother to uncover my lies and that Lumawut could not disprove me either, not having understood what I'd said.

'That's good, my boy,' said the Father. 'Can your father pay the yearly fee of MIM$25,000?' he asked.

I didn't dare take the initiative with that question. I interpreted the Reverend Father's loaded question to Lumawut. He thought for a painfully long while and then asked me to tell the man of God yes.

I had never felt as relieved as I did at that moment. The tables would have turned, and the doors of college education would have closed permanently against me had Lumawut answered otherwise. The church may be about doing good and seeking salvation for the poor, but it needs a little money from the poor to do its job properly, doesn't it?

The Father was pleased and tossed me a copy of the prospectus of college requirements. As I glanced through it most rapidly, he said, 'Bring all of those items you see mentioned in there.'

'Yes, Father.' I was very excited that thanks to college my list of possessions was going to grow substantially.

'Remember that school reopens on the first day of the month of September, the ninth month of the year and the fourth month from Christmas,' he echoed emphatically. I smiled at his mention of Christmas, the Christian feast we had all made our own. When Christmas was approaching not even the dullest child could make a mistake about its date. The Father kept looking at me until I remembered I had something to say.

'I can't fail to remember that, Father. We have a calendar hanging on the wall in our living room. It will be difficult for September first to pass unnoticed.' This explanation did the trick, and I was happy for it.

'Also make sure you cut down your hair before you come to school. I don't want to see such amounts as you have on your head the day you come through the gates of this college to start your studies. Goodbye and God bless you.' He waved us out of his office as another visitor and his daughter arrived at the door.

We had hardly gone out of the school gates when the Father came running after us, surprisingly energetically. We stopped, and Lumawut ordered me to run towards the Father, which I did.

When we caught up to each other, the Father said, 'I forgot to take the deposit of MIM$10,000. It is the only thing that guarantees your place in the college.' He struggled to catch his breath.

And I struggled to keep my stability. I was lucky Lumawut had foreseen a thing like that and was relieved to see bills change hands and Father hastily shake Lumawut's hand.

I was also lucky that in September, I made it to college in time, despite an initial scare. Lumawut and I had trekked to Jengjeng in the hope of finding a lorry to take us to Nsong, but for four days, there was no vehicle. The heavy rains had made the roads too muddy, too slippery and simply too dangerous to ply. The college was reopening in three days, and there was no sign of a motor car anywhere. I ran the risk of losing my place to someone on the Principal's waiting list. Frustrated yet determined not to miss the first day of college, Lumawut decided for us to set off on foot. I was more than grateful, and swore to crown the trek with success.

***

I first sat in class with girls in college. This surprised me very much for I never knew that elsewhere girls were sent to school, and even as far as college. The discovery made me angry about the missed opportunities for my sister Shaka, and I found it difficult to reconcile the reality of my village with what I was experiencing. What was it that made it possible for girls elsewhere to school and impossible for girls in my village to do the same?

I had never spoken to a schoolgirl before, but here I was, sandwiched between girls, and expected to sit and study with them not only for a year, but for five long years. I was too small and too shy for that. Yet the college authorities had assigned me a desk on an island in a vast ocean of bewildering girls. Not only that. My desk was the first and stood far in front, just behind the door of our rectangular classroom of 30 students, seated in rows of five horizontally and six vertically. All the time I had the feeling I was too exposed to the searching eyes behind me, those of the girls in particular, with whom I was more than unfamiliar in a schooling context.

Once in class after the usual morning assembly and devotional prayers, I rushed straight to my isolated desk where I sat quietly down. From there I followed the lessons attentively from start to finish. Never did I take the initiative to speak to anybody, not even when it concerned my pencil or book that a fellow student had borrowed but failed to return. I preferred he kept the pencil or book until something would prick his conscience to bring it back to me. And I answered questions asked without even looking up to see who was speaking to me. If I was asked for something, I gave it without lifting my head. So I usually didn't know who had borrowed what from me.

I remember a particular episode that shook me right down to my roots. Our history teacher had given a certain assignment on the Holy Roman Empire. He wanted it well done, with all the facts and details. My history textbook treated the topic sparingly and was therefore clearly not an option if I wanted an answer that would please the teacher. There was an encyclopaedia in the library that was said to have treated the topic to the right level of exhaustion.

The afternoon of the assignment I went to the library to consult this encyclopaedia. As usual my hands clasped my head and I began to read the portion of the Chambers' Encyclopaedia that spoke about the rise and fall of the Holy Roman Empire. I was completely oblivious of all the going and coming in the library.

I was so deeply involved with my reading that it all happened as a dream. I heard a soft voice call my name. Despite the suddenness, my shyness still managed to keep me from looking up. But the voice that arose from the seat directly opposite mine on the same table reached my ears again with even sweeter gentleness.

'Ngoma Lumawut, kindly excuse me with your pencil.'

I just couldn't believe my ears. Cold sweat rushed into my armpits and wet my shirt. The pencil was lying on the table. I quickly pushed it across to the voice and continued my reading, ignoring a well refined "thank you." The rapid manner in which I pushed the pencil across the table made me feel foolish. The effect was so great on me I hardly distinguished one boldly printed line from another. I read them in a confused and haphazard way. I rushed over the pages and took my leave without saying a word to the girl with the soft voice, but I did glance briefly over my shoulder at her back. I could not understand where the charmingly daring girl had stolen my name, but I could feel myself contradicting myself even as I ran out of the library.

I felt relief as the fresh cold air greeted me. And, despite myself, I convinced myself I would not like to be near her again. I wished she would keep the pencil and not run after me to say "take your pencil, please." I hadn't the nerves to meet her again, much as I felt the urge to see her again. I was too shy and afraid of girls. I realized I didn't know them. I had grown up with an elder sister whom I thought I knew, but it was at college I realised just how little I knew of girls.

It was two days later that I understood the girl was in the same class with me. That was when she brought me back the pencil. Why had she kept it for that long? I wondered. I said thank you and turned away, as abruptly as I was nervous. From the corner of my eye, I saw her smile and go back to her desk which was just a row away from mine. But that was the end of whatever there was between us. She must have grown tired of wasting her greetings and attention on someone built of clumsy indifference. She never understood that deep down in me, where boys are loud and open about their naked truths, I admired her. But I simply hadn't the wits to express my sentiments or even to smile freely at her.

37

My negative attitude towards girls compensated me in one way. It made me very attentive in class. I had time for nobody. Only the teachers interested me. With this attitude it wasn't long before I began to be noticed in class, particularly in Mathematics and French. Right to this day I still don't understand how I came to know these subjects so exceedingly well. I just found myself inexplicably and steadily rising above the rest of my classmates in these two disciplines. The teachers of both subjects became especially interested in me, and my performance in class became the standard of measure. Whenever a test was corrected in either subject, my script was never returned with those of my classmates. It was always kept aside by the teacher as a mirror through which the other students could measure their heights and sizes. Bit by bit I became courageous, and soon, I could stand up and ask questions in class without being intimidated. It was as if doing well in these subjects had injected me with courage and tamed my fears and shyness.

Mathematics and French seemed to be the key subjects in the college. I found that my excellence in them almost automatically gave me a very easy time with the other disciplines. Subjects like English and English literature, History, Geography, as well as the rest of the sciences were scarcely a problem to me. I picked them up with my left hand, as one would say back home to denote that something was easy. This made me grow popular. And this popularity could be seen in the fact that every student in class knew my name, while I could hardly boast of knowing half the names in our class of ninety-six students.

In Form Two, when my excellence in Mathematics was incontestable, and when most of my classmates had been gradually led to accept the unpleasant truth that I was above them, they, and in particular the girls, brought me Mathematics problems to solve for them. The girls liked me because I never took anything for granted. I always went back to the first principles or the roots of their problems, from where I gradually coursed my way to the areas of immediate concern. The same applied to French and other subjects on which I was consulted. Whoever brought a problem to me always went back with an answer and also a general technique for solving similar problems.

There was a girl who occupied the third desk on the horizontal row immediately to the right of mine. We came to know each other in a curious way. This girl had a certain outstanding beauty about her and a peculiar proud way of walking. Her behaviour was different from that of the other girls in our class. She hardly talked to anyone, not because she was shy like me (for she was bold to the eye) – but because she thought herself superior to the rest of us. Her sandals, skirt, blouse, and wristwatch were expensive looking and quite unlike any of the locally made trash most of us were proud to wear. She was unmistakably the student with the most expensive wristwatch among the five students in our class with watches worth writing about. In light of all the rich evidence, I could not dare to mistake her for a peasant like myself. To insult the rich and famous of the land was tantamount to treason. That I knew only too well.

A pompous boy probably from one of the upper forms used to pop in every now and then to see this girl. He used to sit and talk with her for interminable lengths of time. I could hardly guess what they talked about at such length. The big boy was already a well known nuisance in our class. He seized every opportunity, when he found our class without a teacher, to come in and speak for a long time with the girl. One day when this boy had come and gone as he often did, the girl called me and asked, 'Why are you looking at me in that way?'

'I am not looking at you,' I said, all tense.

'Don't lie, Ngoma Lumawut. You have been staring at me for a very long time now. Why?' She was slow and deliberate in her speech, staring me in the eyes.

If I didn't melt that day, I never would, ever, I thought.

'I have told you that I was not looking at you, but you don't want to believe me,' I said and turned back to face the blackboard. But I continued to worry. Why did I turn and stare at this girl unconsciously, for so long a time? I felt ridiculous and ashamed.

Later that day a classmate and one of the rare boys I spoke and laughed with confirmed that I had indeed stared inquisitively at the girl for a long time.

'There must be a reason why you can't take your eyes off her,' he insisted.

I was ill at ease, but I had begun to learn not to care. Was I at long last becoming a bold boy? Not long before then, one of the most boastful boys in our class had arrogantly bleated what he termed his winning formula with girls. Boldness is the beginning of wisdom and a lifetime of achievements with girls, he had said, more or less, and this seemed to have stuck with me.

Things continued normally as I maintained my lead in class. My mates found me an impregnable rock to crack. They tried in vain to beat me many more times than I can count. There were times a student or two scored more than I did in a subject like Geography or History, but I remained the unbeatable man in all the sciences.

Among our subjects only Physics and Cookery had a direct imposed correlation with the sexes. The study of Physics was almost an exclusive privilege of the boys while Cookery was completely associated with the female sex. In Form Two no girl could opt to exchange Cookery for Physics, no matter how interested or how good she claimed to be in the latter. It was harsh but real, these stark choices. On the other hand, boys, almost as if it was written in their genes, were systematically exempted from Cookery, by the school authorities who always insisted they knew best. Both the Cookery and Physics classes were held once every

Wednesday when the last two morning classes were set aside for them. Immediately after the end of the second class every Wednesday morning, the girls took the path to the kitchen as the boys entered the Physics laboratory.

Having imbibed the superior wisdom of the school authorities, the boys looked down on subjects such as Cookery and regarded Physics as something only boys could do. The more difficult a boy found the sciences, the more likely he was to be likened to a girl or said to be doing easy, feminine subjects.

In the kitchen the girls worked under the exclusive supervision of Reverend Sister Esther Blueyes, an Irish woman who was said to have studied food and nutrition to a level of permanent head damage back in Ireland many years ago. The fact that her head was veiled only increased our suspicion that it had indeed been permanently damaged.

She taught the girls how to prepare European dishes and how to observe European table etiquette. After the Reverend Sister had imparted the theory to them, she began practically preparing the various dishes while they watched her. Then came their turn to repeat what she had done. It was only after the girls had become accustomed to basic principles for the preparation of assorted European dishes that the Sister would allow them to prepare dishes of their own taste. Of all the Form Two batches that Reverend Sister Esther Blueyes had taught, she confessed that the girls of our batch outclassed all the others. The girls of our class operated smoothly in the kitchen, artfully mixing and blending foods.

The tradition was for the Form Two boys to rush down to the reception room after their Physics class and eat what female counterparts had prepared during the Cookery lessons. It was for this reason that rumours spread about Form Two being the most privileged class in the school. Stories even went from mouth to mouth of certain boys who had chosen to repeat Form Two to retain the privilege

41

of eating what the girls cooked. At the reception room the boys ate *en masse*. The girls had the option to issue special invitations to schoolmates of their choice, including non-Form Two boys or girls – but few invited girls. It wasn't compulsory that invitations be given out. Girls could keep their food to themselves. After each general meal at the reception room, those who could boast of special invitations stayed behind and waited for the girls who had invited them to come out and take them individually. And all boys looked forward – even the most timid of us – to these special personal invitations.

Something great happened to me one Wednesday morning after the second class. I was searching in my desk for my Physics notebook as my classmates rushed about, when I noticed the rich, proud and stunning girl approach my desk. My heart gave three big thuds and sank. I looked again to assure myself that my eyes were not playing tricks on me, but she stood there, tall and elegant, defying my incredulity.

'Are you not going for the Physics class, Ngoma Lumawut?' asked she, trying to look into my desk. 'What is the matter with you?' she added.

'I can't find my Physics notebook.' I couldn't stop the sweat on my face.

'Is it the search for the book that makes you sweat?' she asked with a sarcastic smile.

'What do you think it is? I badly need the book.' I managed to sound natural.

'Let me help you look for it.' She had stopped smiling to wear a serious helpful countenance.

'No, don't worry, I've seen it,' I said. 'It was lying below my thick Atlas.' I paused for a moment to wipe the sweat off my face. Then I bolted, saying, unconvincingly, 'I am late and I must hurry.'

She came after me and said, 'I believe you think yourself the only one late for class. What do you think I am doing here?'

'What are you doing here, since you asked? Why aren't you going to class?' I asked her with borrowed boldness.

'You are a strange boy, Ngoma Lumawut. You ask the most absurd of questions.'

'I don't see how absurd my questions are,' I said and shook my head to reinforce my doubt.

She smiled and asked me whether I had suddenly ceased to be in a hurry. I made to go but she stopped me again and held out a carefully folded sheet of paper.

'What is that?' I asked.

'It is for you. How do you expect me to know? Read it for yourself,' she said teasingly, with a smile.

'Who gave it to you?'

'I don't know,' she retorted and placed the folded paper in my shirt pocket, and walked away in majestic fashion.

I reached for the paper, which I found and quickly unfolded. It was a special invitation. My eyes went blind for a moment. When they became clear again I expected to find something else written on the paper. But it was there, graceful script inviting me to come and eat her dish at lunch time. She called me a name my classmates rarely used because of its recent adoption. Richard was the additional name I took up when the Principal baptised me at the end of the third term in Form One. The name had been inspired by our history lessons about Richard the Conqueror, although I should have, in accordance with the tradition of the Roman Catholic Church, ideally taken the name of a saint. The invitation read: 'Richard, I have the special pleasure to invite you to come and appreciate my cooking. Kindly stay around at the reception room after the general meal. Thank you. It's me, Collette.'

I read the note over and over again, each time trying to pronounce her name which I was learning to say for the first time. It was too dreamy to be real. I felt weightless and giddy with excitement.

That morning I perplexed my Physics teacher. Questions he thought I would easily answer baffled me. I wasn't as active and sharp as usual. Colette occupied my mind. Her smooth, firm, ebony self dominated my being and every thought. I was transformed into a day dreamer. I could not take notes. The teacher watched me keenly. He roamed the room, looking at our notebooks. Each time I saw him coming, I struggled to copy from the book of a classmate sitting close by. But the teacher soon got my trick.

'What is the matter with you, Lumawut.' He always chose to call me Lumawut.

I stared blankly at him, not knowing what to say.

'Why are you not taking down notes? What is wrong with you today? Are you sick?' The teacher asked me in a fatherly way.

'Yes, Sir, I have a headache,' I lamely accepted.

The other boys all burst out laughing. They could not understand how a boy who had been so active a while ago during the History lesson could suddenly develop a headache to the point of not being able to take down notes in class. But the teacher was deceived. He trusted me enough to be taken in by my lie.

'Yes, yes, you must be. You must be sick. For sure you are. I've never known you to be inactive. You can go down to the dormitory if you like.' He stood right by me and was lightly touching my head.

I was wise enough not to accept the suggestion. Else, what would my mates have said when after the class they found me racing towards the reception room, with a special invitation carefully and proudly displayed in my shirt pocket?

'Thank you very much, Sir, but I prefer to persevere. I don't want to miss the lesson entirely,' I whispered, and my classmates laughed. They knew I was up to something, that much I could feel.

The teacher smiled with satisfaction and continued with his lesson – a lesson I hardly followed. I guess you could say I was into a different realm of Physics. My mind was already in the reception room, waiting along with some of the special invitees after the masses had fought and gone. Anxiety consumed me when I considered that this could be an expensive joke Collette was playing on me. I made up my mind that if it turned out to be the case, I would receive it like a man. But she would be sure to regret all her life playing a joke on me.

There were three boys in my class with whom I had become very friendly. We were almost always together, and we had taken for ourselves the name Four-in-one. That Wednesday after the common meal I hid from them. I didn't want them to throw questioning looks at me, asking me why I was sticking around. Also, I did not want to share my disappointment with others if things turned out badly. If Collette had taken upon herself to play an expensive joke of humiliating me, I wanted my devastation to stay between us two.

I was the first person to pop into the reception room after the mass of boys had retreated. Fear seized me when I saw no other person there. Time seemed to drag itself along on heavy crutches. It took forever for a second face to appear at the door. The boy was tall, huge and very unfriendly. He walked into the room refusing to notice me and stood far away from me with his head turned upwards. It appeared as if he considered it criminal and against his personal norms to look at the floor. While he was still checking out the ceiling another boy appeared at the door. This one I recognised as a self-important classmate of mine. He expressed great shock at finding me there.

45

'Ngoma Lumawut, you too are here? What have you come to do here?' He asked in a mocking manner.

I ignored him. But it worried me all the same that the boy should undermine me to such an extent. It is true that I was among the poorest boys in our class, if not the poorest. Still that was no reason to torment me in this manner. It made me marvel whether it ever occurred to this proud fool that the money he used was not exactly his, but that of his parents and that he still had a long way to go to prove himself through personal achievement. I could recall feeling just as bad and contemptuous, my very first night as a student in the college, when one of the senior prefects had come raiding for "Funky" – the snacks and delicacies specially prepared or bought by parents concerned the college might not feed their children well enough. In my excited ignorance to please, I rushed to my trunk and came back with avocadoes, mangoes, mixed fried corn and groundnuts, boiled smoked sweet potatoes, and other village delicacies my mother had dutifully and delightfully prepared for me to take along. When I presented these to the prefect, I was rebuked in words I have never forgotten: 'What villager is this clown? And what is he taking me for? The chief of his village?' He mocked me, attracting laughter from the urban and well-off students in my dormitory – those with prefabricated tins and packages to satisfy his appetite as a choosy beggar! Subsequently, I would get lots of punishment from the same prefect for walking with both hands in my pockets. He was devilishly clever with his fists and feet, when it came to punching and kicking junior students.

In the reception room, everyone but I seemed to be at ease. I could read from the body language of the other boys that none of them was there for the first time. I was the odd one out and felt as if my legs were going to decompose, as one by one the girls came out and went back with their specially invited boy. I felt like a student caught stealing examination questions from the safe in the Principal's office.

The last boy went in with his hostess. I remained numb in the reception room, until something dazzled in the kitchen door. I blinked my eyes hard and realized it was Colette, the same one who had infiltrated my thoughts in Physics. She came toward me, apologizing for her lateness. I hoped she didn't hear the breath of relief escaping my otherwise motionless self. When she arrived beside me, I felt reactivated. Together we walked into the kitchen, hand in hand, to the great amazement of my vain mates.

She showed me to a chair, placed a plate on the table in front of me, and uncovered the dishes, which she introduced so rapidly that I couldn't retain any of the exotic names I was hearing for the very first time. My mouth watered as I looked at the strange food. She struggled to explain certain things to me but I was not interested, though it would have been very impolite to make her know that. I sent my right hand into one of the dishes and retrieved a bit of the food which I threw into my mouth, making her eyes fall off her head.

'Richard! This is a meal for a fork and a knife!' She spoke with composure, but I sensed an angry scream suppressed.

I apologised. She smiled and placed the fork and the knife in front of me, determined to civilise me. Then she brought her stool nearer and whispering 'bon appétit,' she watched me eat. From time to time I could see a pair of jeering masculine eyes watching me fumble with the obstructing cutlery. Collette seemed a little ashamed at my show of village ways. But I had decided to adopt a carefree attitude. I even consoled myself that these boys were silly to laugh at me, as they had not been born with cutlery in their hands and napkins around their necks. These jeerers of mine laughed out when I finished every last morsel of my meal when, according to them, it was trendy and showed a touch of class to never empty one's plate. Had they never heard of the eleventh commandment: Thou Shall not waste?

After the meal, Collette walked with me back to the class and left me at my desk with thanks that I had appreciated her cooking. And she went back to her desk. My three associates could not believe what they saw. When the girl had gone to her seat, these three friends came and stood around my desk, asking me to explain my moves. They could not comprehend how a wretched son of a village trader like me should walk hand-in-hand into class with as rich a chick as Collette. Just to avoid further disgrace, I promised to explain things to them later.

Collette never invited me again. Once more I became a nameless face in the crowd. What pleased me, however, was that she invited no one else. I knew this because after the general meal, I usually saw her go with the crowd down to the girls' dormitories. I concluded that even if Collette had rejected me because of my lack of table etiquette, she at least had pleased me by not replacing me with a more civilised boy. Our relationship did not progress beyond the monotony of passive greetings at every meeting. Sometimes she brought me a problem in Mathematics which I solved as I did for every other person. My experience with the proud pampered fools in our class had made me sceptical of pushing anything further with Collette. I preferred to avoid disgrace.

My results that year reassured me that I wasn't completely forsaken, even if badly in need of civilisation. I had something too to show the world. I had the head which most of my rich counterparts lacked. For two years now I had succeeded in leading the class every term. This made me proud. Even if I hadn't table etiquette, I could at least boast of examination etiquette. In this vast complex world of ours, everybody has something to boast of, I told myself. Nobody is completely lacking, just as nobody has a monopoly of good qualities.

Chapter Four

When I arrived home for vacation after the end of my second year in college, a big feast was being prepared in our compound. Mother had just given birth to another baby girl. This time Lumawut's reaction greatly surprised Mother, it wasn't as bitter as expected. The presence of the boy who preceded this newborn seemed to have transformed his bitterness into tolerance. Now that he had a successor in the person of my little brother, he was pleased. At the birth of my third sibling, Lumawut decided to organise a big feast to which he invited people dear to him in Bonfuma and the surroundings.

The first person who saw me coming was Shaka, my elder sister. She had grown into a woman in my absence. I thought about how fast people grow and wondered if she thought I too had grown. We all claim to detest death with a passion, yet day in and day out we rush towards it like mushrooms hurrying to be harvested for the next meal. She embraced me and relieved me of the trunk on my head.

'What have you put in this thing that is so heavy, Ngoma?' She asked as she put it on her head.

'There are my books in it.'

'You are going to continue with school during the holidays?'

'No, but I had no place to store them. This holiday is a long one. And we will have to change classrooms when we go back. It is for that reason that our "big man" advised us to leave none of our belongings in school,' I explained to her.

49

'By big man you mean your principal?'

I was surprised by her question. I had never mentioned the word principal to her before, or had I forgotten?

Shaka remarked my surprise and smiled. 'I have been going through the books you left in the house. I hope you don't mind.'

I shook my head to say I was rather pleased.

'I am now in Class Seven,' she laughed. 'Having finished reading your Class Six reader!'

'You've been reading? Who is teaching you to read?'

'No one. I am teaching myself. I don't want any man teaching me how to read and write when they would not let me go to school…'

She went on and on, and I could feel her anger and legitimate bitterness.

'Ah! I almost forgot to ask about your examination results.' She giggled. 'But don't blame me. If you weren't so good one would be anxious to ask. Is it not true what Lumawut says, that your big man writes every now and then, saying that since you came to his college you have never let anyone go ahead of you?'

I laughed off her question.

'Your big man says you drink books like water.'

I laughed again.

'Tell me about your performance this term. Maybe there was a little change of positions.'

I was moving ahead of her, so I shook my head to indicate there was no change.

'You see, it is a mere formality asking about your examinations.' She paused and adjusted the trunk she was helping me carry. 'Tell me, Ngoma, are those boys so foolish that they can never write like you?' There was a baffled expression on her pretty face, which I was appreciating in a fresh new way, since my exposure to girls in college.

I was pleased to note that my elder sister could have held her own with many girls her age in our college, had she been given the opportunity to go to school.

'There are not only boys in the college, there are girls as well.' I ignored her question.

'Girls?' Her surprise could be seen all over her face. 'What are they doing there, Ngoma?'

'Studying, of course! They read hard, as hard as the boys.' I told her.

'Do they understand a thing?' She was quite confused.

'Yes, and sometimes even better than boys though never as much as I,' I said, and smiled uncomfortably, knowing how perplexed my sister was with such contradictions in discrimination.

'I hope the big boys in your school are not bullies,' said Shaka. She had just noticed a scar left by a wound I got playing football.

'No, I am a good boy, and they don't hurt good boys,' I laughed. 'But a few days before we closed this term, I came closest to being punished by a big boy.'

'I'm all ears. What happened?'

'This prefect came to our dormitory, and asked in an expectant and desperate sing-song voice, "Do you have garri?" "No," I replied. "What about sugar?" "No." More desperate than ever, "Don't tell me you don't have groundnuts!" "No." Absolutely disappointed he concluded, "Then you must be a very poor student," and before I could apologise for my poverty, he screamed, "Get out!!" And I ran for my dear life.'

'You've always been a good runner, Ngoma.'

'Garri is not a favourite Funky…,' I paused, not sure whether or not I had shared with Shaka what Funky meant. 'Funky is any food …'

'You've told me that before,' Shaka interrupted.

51

'OK. Garri is not a favourite Funky, but it is very popular at the end of term when all other Funky has been exhausted and students are short on money. These are the rare moments when students with garri are kings. But they soon become unpopular kings if they want to keep their garri to themselves. Sometimes selfish students hide to eat alone. Sometimes they spit into the garri they have soaked in cold water, when they see other students rushing towards them with spoons.'

'That's wicked,' said Shaka. 'And dirty. They want to eat alone? And miss the joy of sharing?'

'That's college life.'

My sister and I had reached the compound, so we decided to postpone our talk as Mother with the new baby and my junior sister and brother came rushing to greet me. All was joy that evening. Mother was particularly happy I had maintained the lead at school.

From Jengjeng, with my trunk, I had trekked the long bushy path that linked that cosmopolitan little town to Bonfuma. The road is long and I feared doing it all alone. So three weeks before vacation the previous year, I wrote to inform my family and ask them to send Shaka to wait for me in Jengjeng. It's with her that I did the long journey. We had interesting things to talk about. But this time I failed to write and inform my people in time and my sister was not present at Jengjeng to receive me. Worst of all, my trunk was heavier this time than last year. All the same I was lucky enough to meet some boys and girls who had come to attend the Jengjeng market. Among them were the young men Lumawut sent to buy three bags of rice. I waited till they had finished with all their selling and buying, then we started home together. My heavy trunk passed from one head to another until we arrived home. Not very far away from our compound, the last of my helpers gave me the trunk and branched off the main path into their own compound. After I had gone quite far with it, my sister appeared and took the trunk from my already painful head.

Lumawut personally roasted a cock to mark my safe and successful return from school. We ate, drank and discussed a lot of things. Happiness descended as a favourite guest of the household and set up residence in every heart. My little brother and sister played round me, caring little that I was carrying their baby sister in my arms. From time to time I tried to explain to them how dangerous it was, playing near a very little baby. But the way they resumed their playing almost immediately after my warning, showed how lightly they took my warnings.

My Mother expressed satisfaction at the way the college cooks were feeding me. She saw nothing to make her accuse my big man of not feeding us well. Before we went to bed at an unusually late hour that night, Lumawut declared that the feast in three days would be doubly significant. It would also be a celebration of my stellar performance for the past two years.

My arrival three days before the scheduled feast was timely. I found myself in the midst of heated preparation. Lumawut had asked a number of young men and women to move into our compound and help until the feast had come and gone. I was asked to share my room with some of these young men until the feast was over. This didn't worry me much as long as they could content themselves with the floor, my bed being a little too good for what I now saw as dirty looking village folks. I had to take great care to avoid carrying lice back to college and becoming laughing stock yet again among the girls and boys of my class.

Each of the remaining days came and passed in serious preparations. Lumawut had negotiated for palm-wine with some of his young associates in Safang. He had been so friendly with them when Mother lived there that he didn't face problems in convincing them to bring wine the day before the feast. The young men still trusted him as a man capable of paying promptly. When the wine was brought, Lumawut mixed it with honey and water. The honey was brought by a friend of his from Ngong-Ngong – a place renowned for its droning bees – where it is very cheap. Lumawut had also bought a hefty bull from his friend Ardo Yaroko Bobo, chief of the Fulani, which he had tied behind the compound to eat grass and fatten until the day it would be slaughtered. Three large bags of rice, a very rare delicacy, were bought in the faraway market of Jengjeng, where the lorry from Nsong always dropped me off.

The feast at last came up on *Nyensa*, the third day that followed my arrival on Saturday. That day, people in our compound rose with the birds. Some of the early risers went down to fetch water from the stream, while others stayed behind to make fire at the various fire places. I didn't feel like rising with them. I was too tired and too conservative with my health. There were after all enough people to do everything without my assistance. I always asked myself the question of what would have happened if I didn't come on holidays. Would the feast not have taken place if it had been scheduled to take place during the school year? My meeting the feast and being made part of it was just a matter of chance. I therefore did not see how the people should suddenly think me so indispensable in a thing that had originally been scheduled without me or thoughts of me. I decided to do what I liked, when I liked.

Mother and Shaka were leading the group of women preparing the fufucorn. They placed big aluminium pots containing milky corn water above the fire places, which had already become hot. When the milky corn water began boiling, the women paired up and took a basket of corn flour to each pot. One of the women sprinkled the flour in the milky corn water in the pot while the other stirred vigorously with a stirring stick. As more flour was added and more vigorous stirring and turning done, the contents of the pot began transforming into solid fufucorn. The stirring continued for long after the mixture was judged sufficiently thickened. This extra stirring was to harden the mixture to make it solid enough to mould into loaves. The loaves were displayed in huge baskets and covered with banana leaves passed over fire for a brief moment to soften. The baskets were carried to tents that had been raised near the general store.

Lumawut and the young men struggled a long while with the bull. One young man stood idly by as the others fought to put down the bull. The animal got loose and caught the idler unawares and pushed him with its horn, on the back, making him fall on his stomach. He was very lucky that Lumawut and the other men saw it in time and rushed to stop the beast from returning. Otherwise the feast would have turned into mourning. The victim was eliminated from the preparations and had to lie on Lumawut's bed after being rubbed with potent ointment.

When Lumawut and the rest of the young men returned to the bull, they were determined didn't struggle for long before killing it. They cut its neck and skinned it with sharp cutlasses. They cut the meat into huge pieces which they cooked in pots as big as those used in preparing the fufucorn. Only a few of the pots used for the occasion actually belonged to Lumawut. The rest were from generous neighbours, to be cleaned and returned after the event. It was difficult for an individual, no matter how rich he claimed to be, to single-handedly organise a feast like this. Even locally rich men like Lumawut – whom I now knew from my college experience wasn't all that rich by the standards of the towns and cities beyond – still needed material support in the form of pots, and spoons and seats, not to mention human hands, free or paid. It is true, the saying that one hand, however endowed, cannot tie a bundle.

When the meat was ready, Mother and my sister came and took over from the men, to finish off the cooking. They added the necessary garnish. Then the meat, ready to be served, was also carried to the storage area in the special place built for the occasion.

By sunrise the first handful of guests arrived with gifts for their host. The gifts were taken away to the storage area as the men were given seats in Lumawut's house. There they were given a calabash of palm-wine mixed with honey to sip while waiting for the feast to begin. The women were shown into Mother's house. But all the gifts, whether by women or men, were kept in one place. Not a single person came without something. The women found it boring sitting in the house doing nothing, so they joined Mother and the young women in their preparations outside. Some asked for the baby girl, and admired her saying that, unlike her immediate elder brother, she looked more like her Mother than her father. Women often like to throw in a comment or two on looks, comments that sometimes reassure, just as they can unsettle the wife or husband, depending on the state of their relationship.

By the time all the food had been cooked, the compound was warming and swarming with people. They came from all over Bonfuma and even beyond. Lumawut was a well known man generally considered very friendly. Mother had been in Bonfuma now for over nine years, but nobody had so far found any cause to fall out with her. She was friendly with women and men together. Lumawut's first wife had simply faded out of the collective memory of the village. Bonfuma was so full of episodes that from time to time an incident or two had to cede its place to a new and more vivid one.

The feasting formally began when the sun had sailed to an overhead position. Though the celebration was taking place in the heart of the rains, Lumawut had made all possible arrangements with the village rainmaker to keep the rain at bay for the whole of that day. In full confidence, the rainmaker boasted he would refund Lumawut's fee if there was as much as a drop of rain that day. Pleased, Lumawut promised to send the rainmaker's share of the feast over to his compound where he would be busy stopping the rain from falling.

Before the feast started, all the guests were asked to occupy the seats that had been assigned them in the open space of the compound. My immediate follower ran into my room and told me that Mother was asking me to hurry up and join them outside before the festivity began. I took a quick bath and joined the others who were already seated in the large space in the middle of the compound. The man I spotted first was my primary school Class Seven teacher, Mr. Samson Samba. He was sitting among the distinguished guests up at the veranda of Lumawut's house. I went up to greet him.

'When did you come back from college, Ngoma? How long have you been here? You just appeared so abruptly,' he said, still shaking my hand which he continued to hold.

'I arrived two days ago, Sir,' I said. 'But I was too tired to come and greet you over at the school.'

'You are changing, Ngoma, you are changing. How can you be too tired to come and greet me, your teacher?'

I could see the disappointment on his face. His grip on my hand weakened and he let go of it. Experience had given him so much confidence in me. I could see him questioning it then. He had never thought me capable of spending the night of my arrival without rushing to him to report my coming.

'I'm very serious, Sir. I've been lying in bed since I came. I've been very weak all this while. Mother will tell you that I'm not lying,' I tried hard to convince him.

'If you thought of me, Ngoma, you would have found a way. Your little sister knows my house. Why didn't you send her to tell me you were too weak to come? It is strange, Ngoma. There is a strange change. That is all I can say, for now.' He folded his arms around his chest and sat.

'I admit it's my fault for not having thought of sending my sister to you. But to tell you that I no longer think of you would be a fat lie.' I stopped to look at him. He stared back at me with a blank expression on his face. 'That can't happen, Sir,' I added, and firmly too.

He threw his hands apart and said with resignation, 'It is all left to you, Ngoma. You are free to do what you like.' He seemed to think for some time, then, in a gesture of forgiveness, he told me to forget about it.

I felt relieved, for he was the last person in the village to whom I would want to be indifferent.

'But tell me...,' he held my hand again, in a friendly and caring way. 'Were your results still excellent this time?'

'I came first again, Sir,' I told him, with a broad smile.

Mr. Samba looked worried. He had a thing that troubled him in his mind. Lumawut was getting into the middle of the compound to address the seated crowd. I made to regain my original position, but Mr. Samba asked me to sit by him. Before Lumawut began addressing the people, Mr. Samba warned me.

'Be careful not to be deceived by your excellent performance into cultivating pride. You never know what may turn up in this world. Pride might bring you untold problems. I prefer your simple and humble self of two years back.' Before he stopped to let Lumawut speak uninterrupted, Mr. Samba whispered to me that we should adjourn our talk until later when I came to his house to formally report my arrival home on holidays.

Lumawut was putting on a *dala* gown woven for him by an aged specialist who lived at a village southwest of Bonfuma. To complete his dressing, he tied round his waist two large pieces of the same specially woven cloth. These pieces of cloth took the place of trousers or a pair of shorts, and suited the gown well, giving Lumawut a very elegant look. It brought to mind the image of a Scotsman in his kilt which I first encountered in my first year English reader at college. Lumawut stood at a strategic point from where he could see and be seen by the entire crowd. That was the first time ever to the best of my knowledge that Lumawut was standing to address a gathering. I listened with sharpened ears.

He cleared his throat and began to speak.

'I am immensely gratified that you have honoured me by coming in numbers. It makes me very proud to know that the one-handed man may still hope to have his bundle of firewood tied for him in this community. There is nothing more reassuring...' He paused as the crowd, liking what they heard, interrupted with applause.

'In the past I struggled all alone with my own bundle,' he resumed. 'It is special or personal luck if I succeeded. Lately, I thought it is better to share my successes and failures with the community. The community that gives me strength and guides me along life's narrow path...'

There was applause again, which he acknowledged by gracefully bowing to the crowd.

'A good boy is the one who brings home his catch to his father. It gives the boy much pleasure if the father can appreciate his effort. The father may spit blessings on the catch and return it to the son. He may take the whole of it, leaving his son only with the tail. But whatever the case, the son shuns all grudge against his father, because the ways of the land hold it that the judgement of the father stands irrevocably supreme, above that of his son, no matter the son's intelligence. According to the custom, a son can never be wiser than his father, for it is the father who decided what portion of wisdom to lend to his son.'

The notables agreed and applauded as they shook their heads. Not much clapping came from amongst the women and the children, this time. But this was hardly noticed, as the notables were loud and noisy in their response.

Lumawut continued, 'I have been living with a woman for a long long time now...'

This time it was the turn of the women to interrupt him with loud applause and ululations, interspaced with the calling of Mother's name.

Both Mother and Lumawut acknowledged the recognition, and he continued, a broad smile on his face.

'When I brought her here you didn't know. Now I have added three children to the two she had before coming into my house. All these children you don't know. I have sent a son to a college. This asks for almost all the money I toil and sweat for yearly. That too you don't know. In the past I have acted single-handedly, hardly thinking that the genuine taste of palm-wine can never be known to one who hides and drinks it in his bedroom alone.'

Again the crowd responded, in unison with applause and ululation. The notables seized the opportunity to empty their horn cups and asked for more palm-wine sweetened with honey. This was served them promptly, by the male attendants whom Lumawut had instructed to ensure no drinking horn was left unattended.

'I've called you here today to bring my entire family home to the village in a formal way. For when I was a boy still young and innocent – or so I thought – my father told me something I have not forgotten, especially these past four months. He told me that there can be no roots for anyone, if there is no family or community to which one feels committed. Even the birds of the sky must perch from time to time to refuel, before taking off again. How much more of us humans? A family is a family only from the unity it displays, and only with such unity can anything be achieved, individual or collective...'

There were outbursts of applause again, in recognition for the wisdom of the words transmitted by his father, who, at that very moment, seemed to be speaking through his son.

'It is because I have grown to realise the indisputable truth in my late father's words that I have called you here today to share with you the source of my roots. I will introduce each and every member of my family, and ask of you to share with them the blessings of our ancestors and the promise of our land.' Lumawut paused and called for Mother to come forward with the children.

There was defending applause and ululation as Mother stood up. The women showered her with praise song, poetry and ululation.

I remained still until Mr. Samba reminded me to join Mother and my siblings who were already in the middle of the crowd with Lumawut. Lumawut asked me to stand between my junior sister and Shaka. We were placed in order of seniority, except our youngest sister who had to be carried by Mother because she was too young to use her legs. Lumawut began his epic introduction with Mother and went down until his youngest daughter.

Holding Mother's right hand he said, 'This is the mother of my children. She is the remarkable daughter of a leading notable from the high mountains up in the heart of our land. Her kin are resident in the great village of Safang, where all our palm-wine is tapped...'

The whole compound interrupted him with resounding cheers. They understood his words profoundly. In Bonfuma, they drank wine thanks to the efforts of the great tappers of the royal raffia bushes up the mountains. They clapped loud and long as they thought of the physical and mental satisfaction the wine gave them, and to drive the point home, the notables emptied their horn cups and asked them to be refilled. But the crowd also clapped for Mother who was still wonderfully charming after five solid births. So the claps that sprung from the crowd were doubly significant.

When people became silent once more Lumawut took up his words again. Talking about Shaka he said, 'This is the very first fruit she bore in the world. A fruit that came out to resemble the parent tree so remarkably. She followed me to Bonfuma as a small girl, but now she is ripe enough to cause a scuffle among young men!'

The whole assembly roared at his befitting humour. The humour was very apt at a time when some young men were going to taste of Shaka's cooking. It took long for the roars to die down. When at last they did, it was my turn to be introduced. Lumawut held up my hand and showed me round the crowd.

'This young man is the one who has gone to learn so we may be cured of our original blindness that makes us see as if we didn't have eyes. He will lead us away from the floods of the rivers of dimness. He came with the mother of my children, but he has gone furthest of them all. He is at college in Nsong.'

The clapping was long and deep, roaring like the sound of a waterfall. Shouts of support sprouted out from the crowd like mushrooms around a pile of cow dung. They cried out that the ancestors may clean and brighten my eyes for the glory of the land.

When Lumawut came to my only brother after the rapid introduction of my little sister, he had solid affirmations.

'This is the foundation of the Lumawut household,' he announced. 'He is, in terms of tradition, the successor-to-be, hence his name, Ndinda. He will live to continue what I've started. He is the fruit a young husband expects to harvest in his wife when he sows a seed. Know him from today as the one who will answer to Lumawut when you call for me in vain. The girls may pass on to make the glory of other men, but the boys are made to stay and be glorified.'

People shook their heads in understanding and waited for the last introduction which was as brief as the fourth.

Then Lumawut declared the festivity open in the name of his entire family.

We all moved toward the general store, and the food went round rapidly. Men ate to their fill and drank in abundance. There were enough kola nuts to flavour the palm-wine for everybody and to make even women and little children love to take a cup or two. The men broke up into little intimate groups and from time to time asked for an empty calabash to be refilled, while the notables continued to benefit from privileged attention. Containers with lumps of juicy meat passed from notable to notable until they all cried out they could eat no more.

The young boys organised themselves and disappeared into nearby bushes. They reappeared soon after with their little masked dancer called Funinindong. They sang Lumawut's praises, calling him Besogyhah – father of their mate. My young brother joined the group and they danced about the compound together. They were given a lot of food along with a calabash of wine, and a live fowl. They danced on for a little longer and disappeared into the bushes again, this time to eat what they had been offered, and to celebrate their recognition and acknowledgement by the notables.

When at last the women brought their *Njang* to close the feasting, there was still enough food to keep everybody actively involved. The drum beat, the gong sounded and the trumpet echoed the melodious voices of the women who had perfected the art of social commentary through song and dance. Blood rushed to men's legs and they itched to dance the *Njang*, the way they would itch to eat their favourite meal by the loving hands of the mother of their children. One by one the men suspended their drinking and joined the singing and dancing women on the floor. Lamps were brought and stationed to keep the impending darkness in check. Men and women locked themselves under a common emotion as the *Njang* mounted in force. The music and dancing continued far into the night. Few needed convincing that the spirits had joined in with divine invisible voices and instruments. Before it all ended with a heavy downpour, as if the rainmaker had fallen asleep, my heavy eyes took me as well off to sleep.

***

The feast that had been concluded at the beginning of the holiday was still fresh in my mind almost three months later, as a thing of yesterday. Many things that happened after it had been forgotten already. But memories of the feast stayed on. Once in a while my mind was forced to see an analogy between the Son of Man's Last Supper with his Apostles, and the feast Lumawut had offered the people of his village and his friends from neighbouring villages. Every time I was forced to that analogy, I brushed it aside as the dangerous prangs of the creative imagination of a young mischievous mind. It may be the feast stuck to my mind simply because it had been grand, or because I felt guilty about not having been fully and actively involved. People had confessed that history could not claim a feast so grand in Bonfuma. Memories of the feast, laced with joy and worry, gripped me stubbornly and wouldn't let go. Why did they persist even when I had brushed them aside and justified them by my lack of active participation?

Among the children Lumawut had with Mother, the boy was the most outrightly privileged. He was the only one who ate from the same dish with his father. I was now a big boy, but could scarcely remember when Lumawut ever invited me to eat with him. But here was a little boy hardly four years old, already used to privileges that even grown ups struggled to have. It made me wonder whether my own biological father would have treated me with the same

64

outspoken tenderness if he had been with me. Even though my junior sister didn't complain openly, she did so in her behaviour. She sometimes refused to do certain activities asked of her, and when asked why she refused, she would give no reason. To me this implied she was opposed to Lumawut's preferential treatment of her younger brother. He was unconsciously moulding a future fighter. I sensed he ignored dangers involved, though even if he didn't, he would not have changed.

One morning, a day before my scheduled departure back to college, a short woman with watery eyes strayed into our compound in the manner of a wayfarer. She was carrying a girl of about four, strapped to her back with a large towel – a child so light in complexion that one could mistake her for not being her daughter. The woman and her child reminded me of a Fulani woman doing her round of the village with a large gourd exchanging milk and butter for money and foodstuff. The woman carried a small head load of clothes, and on her left hand was a pair of worn plastic slippers that smelt like the fart of a dog gone hunting without its owner. Lumawut who had returned from an unknown journey the day before was conspicuously absent. The woman and her baby were received with all hospitality by Mother. She gave them some of the food she had just prepared, but avoided asking the woman any searching questions.

When Lumawut returned, he told Mother in very brief terms that the woman who had just arrived was his new wife, and that henceforth Mother was to manage only one of the one-room dwellings along with her bigger house. The new woman would have to cook in the other and sleep in his house until her own house was built.

Somehow I had the feeling that Lumawut may not need to build a new house for his new wife. Once more I couldn't stop myself from thinking that this was the beginning of the end of the harmony, however bumpy, that had characterized Lumawut's relationship with Mother. The harmony that many people had wished might stay and serve as inspiration to others.

Lumawut gave me the money to pay fees. The previous two years he had accompanied me to college with the money and paid the fees himself directly to the bursar. I pondered over the matter, affected by the fear that trouble might be just a stone's throw away. What would happen were he, all of a sudden, to decide to discontinue the payment of my fees at college? I shuddered at the thought, but it persisted.

Chapter Five

'Richard, there is some rice and stew in the kitchen behind the house. You may eat all of it if you can. Meet me in front of Mr. Newton Lawson's house along the other row of houses after your meal. It is the third house...'

I interrupted my French teacher. 'I know Mr. Lawson's house very well. He is the new Physics teacher who came to replace the fraudulent one that ran away with a month's salary. You can't know that one, but he taught us Physics till the end of Form Three. I remember how he was very fond of me in Form Two.'

'I don't know the fraud, Richard, but I have heard the shameful story about his outrageous behaviour,' said my French teacher.

'That is why the Principal has grown to be very sceptical of young adventurers like you. He fears that young men who have just left high school come around just to earn enough money to win an entrance ticket into some university out of the country. Did he not torment you when you first handed him an application to teach French in the college?'

'He tossed me up and down for two whole weeks, and when I was about to give up, he told me he was recruiting me on the condition that I respect my contract and the school girls. I would like to ask you, Richard, if you think that is possible.' He was looking me directly in the face.

'What, Sir?' I didn't understand what he meant.

'I mean whether you think it is possible for me to stay with my hands between my thighs, not going behind these

67

girls, some of whom are so charming?' There was a smile on his face, probably intended to deceive me that he was not serious.

'I can't know, Sir, but I follow none of the girls.' I deliberately told the teacher a lie.

'To me, it is practically impossible to teach here without chasing these girls.'

'But there are many beautiful girls around Kibonbong town. Why can't you keep one of them – even if just on a temporary basis – and avoid a lot of problems?'

'And leave these young succulent girls to whom? To you people? But you just confessed how you have no interest in them. If all your colleagues profess such a lack of interest as you, don't you think that the girls would really be dying for men?' His question was accompanied by a deep and broad smile which developed into laughter when he noticed how much what he said made me almost die of laughter. After laughing with me for a minute or so he asked me to hurry up.

'Finish eating quickly, and meet me at Mr. Lawson's.' I will be there playing drafts with him. There is a serious errand I want you to run for me,' he said and we went out of his place together. He went straight up the path to Mr. Lawson' house, while I turned left to the kitchen behind the house.

I dished out some rice and emptied the stew from the pan. With my plate, I settled onto a bench under a mango tree next to the kitchen. While I downed my meal, my mind focused on the teacher's errand. I figured it had to do with a girl, but just which girl remained the question. I concluded he would not have decided to delegate me if the girl in question wasn't one I knew well. I therefore deduced it must concern a girl in my class, one with whom I could easily transact a fast affair on behalf of my French teacher. The problem therefore had narrowed to knowing who this classmate of mine could be. In the early afternoon with all the bright sunshine outside, I somehow felt myself trembling with undefined anxiety. My appetite abandoned me as soon as I understood that his offer of food was not an innocent gesture.

The two teachers were so deeply involved with the drafts that neither noticed me walk up. It was only after I whispered a 'good morning, Sir' that Mr. Lawson who seemed to be winning looked up.

'Welcome, Richard,' said Mr. Lawson. Then he asked me with feigned surprise. 'But why is it that you always sneak in here? Do you think that when the college authorities decree the teachers' quarters out of bounds, they mean it for every class but Form Four?' he joked.

'Newton, don't you know that the Principal fears me?' My French teacher, who was called France by his colleagues, asked with laughter. 'All my friends in the school have a right to defy the college decrees as far as it concerns coming to my house. Richard is the best among my friends in the college. I'm determined to bring him here even when the Principal is sitting in my house ready to catch straying students. And dare he reproach my friend...!' He interrupted himself and laughed off the rest of his words.

I wasn't flattered when he termed me his best friend. Not that I contested the possibility, but any other boy in my present circumstances – about to do the teacher a big favour –, could easily pass for a best friend or whatever platitude he thought he needed to encourage the student to do his bidding. The student could pass for the best among the best of friends, as long as he was willing to run the errand in question.

'Give me a moment, Richard. Just a little time to show this man that I too can play drafts,' the teacher told me, his usual smile on his face.

'You can never beat me, France, not even when I play blindfolded. Right now I can put away all others and still win you with two draft seeds only.'

69

Even though Mr. Lawson said that with a playful smile, I could see he meant every bit of what he said. Mr. France didn't play like one capable of beating even a beginner.

'Drafts is nothing but a boring pastime for me. If it were the game of chess I could beat you like heavy rain on a day old chick,' Mr. France attempted a punch-back.

'I'm not interested in empty noise. Have you the chess game in your house?' Mr. Lawson asked, taking his head so near France that he looked provocatively at his chin from below.

'Who in the whole of this backward area can play chess? Don't you know that chess is not a game for primitive people?' my French teacher managed to say, trying to hide the shame all over his face.

'If you had the chess board here with you, we would have understood whether it is for a primitive man like me or not. Now that this game is simply a figment of your imagination, how can you ever realise your dream of beating me?' he chuckled. 'So go and eat shit as Achebe prescribes,' he went on, throwing down on the board the drafts seeds.

The two teachers asked me to come along with them into the house. Mr. Lawson offered me a bottle of Special Beer, but I declined it because I had never drunk beer. He replaced it with something sweet and told me I wasn't man enough. Mr. France took a bottle of Manawa which he opened and drank in gulps. His colleague opened for himself the Special bottle I rejected.

After he had taken two gulps, Mr. France wiped his mouth and spoke to me.

'What about the dance at the Kibonbong Moon & Star Community Hall tonight. Are you attending or not?' he asked.

'I would have loved to if I had the money,' I told him.

'I know your problem with money, Richard,' he said, nodding his head. Then turning to Mr. Lawson, he said in

French, 'Voici un garçon très intelligent. Mais malheureusement, les parents sont trop pauvres pour lui faire continuer ses études.'

'Oui, je sais, je sais très bien. Ce sont des choses qui arrivent,' Mr. Lawson answered.

'Richard,' Mr. France called me as he put his hand into his trouser pocket. 'I have five hundred MIM dollars to give you,' he said, giving me the money. 'But it is not for you alone.'

My heart sank, not because I wanted the money alone, but because in a while I would know just what sort of mess I was in.

'The money,' he continued, 'is for you and a certain girl I want you to bring to that dance.'

Shocks rippled in me as the teacher went nearer to mentioning the name of the targeted girl. I felt doom, without quite being able to put my finger on why.

'The girl in question is a classmate of yours, very well known for that matter. I don't envisage you are going to face problems meeting her.'

I asked myself why this man was deliberately increasing tension by keeping the girl's name. Just what exactly was he up to? I tried to keep my calm, but it was a tall order. He continued in his slow offensive manner.

'Her name...,' he went, as shock waves reverberated in me, 'her name is Collette. You know her, don't you?'

I did not answer Mr. France. I didn't even hear his question, which could well have been in French or his mother tongue. The name Collette had sent my eyes whirling. Sweat gushed from me, making my shirt as wet as if I had taken a shower with my clothes on. I went blind to everything around me, but for tens of twinkling red stars. Confusion alighted and took hold of my entire being. I was too lost to search for what to say to Mr. France. When at last I managed to look up, my eyes stung with tears which I fought back.

71

'What is the matter, Richard?' My France asked, noticing the transformation in me with concern.

'Nothing but one of my numerous attacks of malaria, Sir.' I told him a lie.

He rushed to his room and came back with two strange looking tablets. He forced me to take one immediately; the other, he asked me to keep till after supper. But my problem wasn't really malaria or when to take tablets. It was about the girl he asked me to bring to the dance.

I called him in a shaky voice and asked with added respect, 'Suppose this girl says she is not going to attend the dance, what do I do?'

'I want you to bring her there. She can't refuse. Bring her by hook or by crook.'

'You are making things unnecessarily difficult for this boy, France.' Mr. Lawson intervened after studying me. 'The confident way in which you say she must come makes one wonder if she isn't your girl already. And if she is, don't you think it will save this guy a lot of trouble if you put your money in an envelope along with a short note expressing with the authority of a proud owner that you want to go dancing with her tonight?'

I thanked God for sending a messiah to my rescue, but my relief was short-lived.

Mr. France didn't seem to be ready for such arrogant and unwarranted intrusion from his sarcastic colleague. He wrapped up his anger in a cold leaf of silence which made Mr. Lawson all the more slow to read it.

'But how have you come to love women so much, man, when at Christ the King College you were all boys, and there was never a girl at Mimboland Protestant College either?' asked Mr. Lawson, sincerely baffled, it seemed to me.

'I hope you don't want to tell me that in these two schools students are not allowed to go on holidays? And have you forgotten that Christ the King is "God's favourite hunting ground"?' Mr. France asked, controlling his mounting anger. Giving Mr. Lawson no time for further interference, he told me to go and do as I had been asked.

I left completely dejected, my legs almost about to melt like candle sticks consumed by a hungry flame.

I found Collette in class copying my history notes for me. Since the beginning of Form Four when I was appointed the college sports prefect, my class attendance became irregular. When I was absent in class, I was sure to be at the Games Room washing or supervising the washing of football jerseys. The work was cumbersome, but I didn't mind it. The prestige and privileges I got from being the sports prefect were many and various. For one thing, access to the Games Room which was situated at a distance from both the boys' and the girls' dormitories meant I could afford space of my own to meet with Collette away from the prying eyes of rumour mongers and trouble seekers. This was convenient for us, as our dormitories were out of bounds to the opposite sex. Collette took great pains to copy my notes whenever she was free. She had the key to my desk and could take or put anything into it in my absence. But most of the times she had to leave rather than take, because I was very poor and could hardly afford a gift for her. On the other hand, I went to her desk almost every day, either when she told me there was something for me in it, or when I wanted a pencil, pen or an extra exercise book, things I never seemed to have when they mattered.

She was so serious with the notes that she didn't notice me until I was already standing over her desk. She stopped writing as soon as she saw me, and lifted her arms to embrace me. There was nothing for us to fear in such an act because it was Saturday, a free day when only overcharged students could be seen on campus. On Saturdays, students were free to go to town to buy extra provisions and other necessities.

At night there was usually a film show, except when the students had decided to organise what was generally known as socials.

This particular Saturday was a special one in that the students had been permitted to attend a dance organised in town by the Catholic Women's Association, to raise funds to help in the building of our college auditorium. Since Thursday, there was serious preparation going on all over the school for this mega event. Boys and girls together were getting ready to show their best attires. Even the very poor boys went to their friends to borrow money, a shirt, trousers or a pair of shoes. They were simply determined to overcome frustration and enjoy the occasion.

I kept aside every scruple and gave Collette a warm embrace and a nice brief kiss. Then I became sullen once more. She noticed instantly that something was the matter. She was very good at noticing.

'What is wrong Richard? You haven't finished preparing for the dance? Is there anything lacking? ...Tell me, Richard....' Her questions succeeded one another with anxious breathlessness.

'There is nothing lacking, Collette. But there is a problem....' I didn't finish what I was saying before she almost pounced on me like a cat on a rat.

'Don't tell me you are not going to the dance! Fever, headache, stomachache or whatever ache! You are going to the dance, Richard!'

'I am not ill, my dear. And it is not that I lack anything either. The problem is at a completely different level.'

I could see her initial anger and frustration giving way to confusion. I wanted her to calm down considerably before showing her the money the French teacher France had given me to bait her to the dance. When I had convinced myself she was calm enough to receive my story, I removed the twisted five hundred MIM dollar notes from my hind pocket,

74

still taking all my time. Collette almost giggled at the sight of the crumpled note. She must have thought it my meagre effort to repay her fabulous expenses on me. But if she did, she must have been foolish because I failed to see what would have been problematic in trying to do her a single good turn in return. I tried to be as solemn in my speech as possible.

'This is the money Mr. France gave telling me to bring you to the Moon & Star for the dance tonight.'

'Wha - a - at! Mr. Wha - a - at?' She was terribly rattled by what came out of my lips. Her immediate reaction after her expression of utter shock was to cover her face with her hands and cry. She cried and cursed for fifteen minutes, which seemed as long as an hour. I didn't know what to do, but I decided to maintain silence as long as she cried, rather than trying to say something that might make the situation even more unbearable. When she looked up again, her eyes were swollen but piercing. She looked as fiery as Count Dracula's latest bride.

I felt unjustifiably guilty. The question she asked made me all the more confused.

'What do you mean, Richard? What do you mean by bringing that rumpled note to make a fool of me?'

'Making a fool of you isn't and has never been my intention, Collette. Please bear with me, darling, understand my circumstances. Mr. France is behind all this. He commissioned me with the supreme authority of the French teacher that he is, and I had little choice. He probably didn't know that you belong to me, and I hadn't the nerves to tell him. Understand me, darling.' I pleaded.

'Nerves indeed!' Collette mocked. 'Since you came to this college your major problem has been nerves! When will you ever develop the nerves to stand up for yourself?'

Giving me no time to answer, she continued speaking.

'Go and tell that monkey that his eyes are definitely misdirecting him. Tell him I tolerate him in class with difficulty and would certainly never even in my wildest dreams venture out with him. Give him back his wealth to keep for girls of his type. Tell him I'm your girl! Tell him that, Richard! Go! Go now!'

The authoritative and firm manner in which she diminished me revealed an aspect of her character that had successfully gone unnoticed during our more amorous, thrilling and harmonious rendezvous.

'Be a little realistic, darling.' I made my voice sound sure, sweet and gentle. 'Can't you see the danger that lies ahead of us? There is danger not only in refusing to accompany him to the dance tonight, but also in making him know your disgust for him.'

I paused for a while as an idea brightened up my mind. It occurred to me that I could use my feigned malaria to my advantage. The teacher would believe me if I told him that the malaria had made it impossible for me to attend the dance. Collette and I could stay behind and enjoy each other's company, if only she would cooperate.

So I suggested to her, 'There is an easy way out of this dilemma, Collette. We can avoid all these problems by both staying behind while the others go dancing. I mean as you've totally refused to accompany the "monkey" to the dance.'

'Do not mock me, Richard. Tell that man what I've told you, and be prepared to go to the dance with me! Do not dare play any trick on me!' I could tell her warning carried the raw materials of a disaster. I knew only too well not to insist any further.

Collette put the exercise books resolvedly into her desk, locked it and told me that at exactly seven p.m. she would be at our usual meeting place, for me to take her to the dance. Then she hurried out as if to crush any excuse squirming in me before it reached my mouth. And indeed she stifled my last desperate attempt to make her change her mind.

Sitting down at her desk, I pondered the whole matter. Then I decided to dismiss without the slightest hesitation the ridiculous words and monkey business she had insisted I transmit to Mr. France. It would be total madness for him to receive those sharp daggers from me. I also dismissed the idea of solving the problem by staying away from Collette and letting her go to the dance alone. She was too nice a girl for me to lose. Having concluded that any solution I envisaged was dangerous, I tried to look for the one that entailed the least danger. I came by it and went to let the teacher know it. An irrevocable conclusion had already been sealed with Collette. There was still some glimmer of light from the direction of the teacher. To his house I went, intimidated and propelled by hope.

Mr. France promptly opened the door as if he had been waiting all the time for my knock.

'Have you seen her?' he asked almost immediately after the door was opened.

I cleared my throat and said yes.

'What has she said?' I could hear a mixture of hope and anxiety in his voice.

'That she is sick and cannot attend the dance,' I told him, and began fumbling in my pocket for his crumpled notes.

'Why didn't you leave it with her all the same?' he asked, extending his hand to collect the money I tentatively held out.

'She asked me to bring it back to you since she will not be going to the dance,' I falsely explained.

'Of what is she sick?'

'She didn't say, Sir.'

He left me at the door and went to his bedroom. He returned with a hundred and fifty MIM dollars that he gave me to pay my way to the dance. I was about to go my way when more trouble fell at my feet.

'Richard, I had almost forgotten. There are some two girls whom I will want you to be with the time I'll not be with them. I am the M.C. of today's dance and cannot have all the time I would have loved to have. Do you understand?'

'Yes, Sir,' I answered. With a man of his dictatorial proportions, I knew well enough not to bother with problems of my own.

'Be there as early as you can before the dance kicks off.'

I left his house a second time that day, even more oppressed with painful throbbing thoughts.

Chapter Six

The first person we recognised in the Moon & Star was M.C. France, our tormentor, our French teacher. He was standing on the platform with a big microphone held close to his chest, embraced with both hands. He wore a navy blue suit said to look like the uniform of the high school students at St. Michael's College in Mbilimbili. His microphone crackled alternately in English, pidgin, French and what he insisted was another European language, which only he could speak and understand. People began wondering whether the dance had been replaced with a stage clown. Somebody, probably the chairman of the occasion – judging by his fashionable clothes – went and whispered something in his ear that brought his babbling to an immediate halt. Before leaving the platform the supposed M.C. removed from the pocket of his coat a twisted piece of cloth in the form of a handkerchief, with which he mopped the sweat from his face. Collette laughed and took my left hand which she caressed with tenderness. I found two seats at a dark corner of the hall. There Collette and I sat and watched the floor being opened by those specially invited as patrons of the occasion.

When Mr. France left the platform he went out of the hall but soon returned with two fat girls stuffed into tight clothes. He seated them somewhere directly opposite us and began to search around the hall. I guessed he was looking for me and asked Collette to excuse me. I walked up to him. He stood with hands akimbo and gave me a superior good evening. I had often heard that people in suits are very condescending to those who hadn't the means to rise to their illustrious lapels. He asked me whether Collette had finally overcome her illness, and I lied to him that I couldn't know, not having seen her again since I left his place. His smile first made me wonder whether he knew more than I thought he did. But after some reflection, I concluded that the smile was just another show of his superiority complex. Second, he could not have been looking around for me if he had seen us arrive.

He took me to the section of the large hall where drinks were being sold and gave me two bottles of Kingsize to carry to his girls with stony looking painted faces. He asked me to keep them company in his absence, providing animation within the strict limits of his prescriptions. I gave the girls the beers and sat with them for sometime. Their company was stifling, and I excused myself partly because of that, but largely because I was sure that Collette must be sullen. Once back with her, I murmured my apology, but she caught me like a wild fire.

'What did you go see that fool for, Richard?' she asked me furiously. 'What did I tell you this afternoon about that monkey?'

'Sorry, Collette. I forgot to tell you that he told me he would be too occupied this evening, and begged me to give those girls over there….,' I pointed to where the two fat girls were sitting, 'the company they need.'

'Richard, that job is too mean for my boyfriend! Stay away from it and cease to be a slave to any monkey! I'm not going to allow you to do such mean and menial things as carrying beer to and keeping prostitutes company!' She was emphatic in her speech.

'Collette, dear, can't you understand that the monkey is too occupied? It is just a little help he asked of me.'

'It doesn't matter. You are with me, he knows that now. Why should he keep you occupied when he knows you have your own female company? Let me not catch you over there again. And dare he stray across here! I will teach him better techniques of climbing up trees in the forest.'

I realised it was sheer waste of time trying to dissuade Collette from a pre-established state of mind. Though I resigned from persuading her and sat by her side, my mind was deep in thought, looking for new ways of overcoming her and satisfying my challenge – Mr. France.

The floor had been opened and people now freely danced with one another. Both men and women sought dancing partners from the opposite sex. But some men or women who found it difficult to acquire partners could be seen dancing in groups among themselves. The first two records were the latest makossa releases. Collette danced both of them with me.

At an interruption by our famous M.C., we sat down to wait for the next set of records. Collette excused herself and went over to where drinks were sold. She didn't need to ask me for my choice, for she knew I took anything non-alcoholic. I took advantage of her temporary absence and rushed across to the two fat girls I was babysitting for the busy Mr. France.

'Wusai you don bi all this tam?' one of them asked me, in immaculate pidgin.

'Dancing over that way,' I pointed to a different direction from where Collette and I were sitting.

'Masa France don as wusai you deh. We tok fo yi se we no sabi fo seeka you bi jus tok se you di go come nana,' said the other.

'Do you need more beer?' I asked them.

'Wait small tam. Hi don jus gi we some nana so. We nova start for drinkam sep,' said the first.

'I am going to dance with my mates. Look for me on the dancing floor if you need anything and want me to bring it to you,' I told them.

'But no music di play nana.' The second of them looked at me with surprise. 'Weti you di go dance with you friend dem?' she asked.

'There will soon be music when Mr. France has finished addressing the hall. I can see that many people are already saturated with what he has been saying. A good enough sign for him to halt his oration. Meanwhile, I'm going to assure my friends because they didn't believe me when I said I would be coming to dance with them.' Giving them no chance for further questions, I dashed off and was soon missing in the crowd of would be dancers frustrated by Mr. M.C. France's self-important utterances.

Collette was waiting for me, two bottles of drinks in front of her. There was a small bottle of Fanta and a bigger one of Special beer. I didn't know for whom she bought the latter, as neither of us took beer. Even before I finished asking myself why she brought the beer, Collette placed the bottle in front of me, telling me it was my drink.

'Why have you bought beer for me, darling?' I asked.

'Don't you see what is written on the bottle? The beer is specially brewed for the handful of soft men who cannot drink stronger brands. I have bought it for you because it is not good that while a woman is lifting a bottle of Fanta to her lips, you are there with a similar bottle, disgracing your manhood to the fullest. The beer is only to remove disgrace, especially when we consider that the percentage of alcohol in it is so low. So, this is a beer only in name. Plus, Special is for someone special. Won't you drink it, my special?'

And that is how I fell into her trap. After drinking a third of the bottle, I was already a transformed man. My eyes grew bigger and the objects I saw diminished with drastic rapidity. My hair stood on end like that of one who had seen a ghost, and I felt as if my blood was overheating and stretching my veins, rendering me bold and excitable. I suddenly became so bold that if the school Principal and Father had been present, he would have known for the first time that God hadn't made me to be a one-phase man as he always thought. Sobriety was not my only quality. I was also capable of the complete negation of it. Thanks to Special, I was soon to discover I was one of many phases and faces.

I abandoned Mr. France's prison and regretted having been so foolish to have yielded to all his caprices. If I had gone back to the fat ugly fools, I would have told them the truth about themselves and dramatised my superior status as a student from the most reputable college in the region. But luckily, they didn't see me again nor I them. I devoted myself to Collette, *my* someone special. I danced with her from then till the end of the gala, and at the centre of the hall where hundreds of eyes focused on the most daring and beautiful. No sensible man unsure of his partner's splendour could dare disgrace himself by proceeding to the centre of the hall. I danced every song – whether blues, makossa, reggae or disco – with Collette, thoroughly engrossed in her.

People watched us and our modern tendencies, full of marvel. We demonstrated how it was impossible to exhaust innovations in the field of love. Neither the sober Collette nor the intoxicated Richard paid attention to all the stares and commentary around us. The effect of the beer was tremendous. I damned all situations, conditions, and people. People became smaller every time I tried to look at them. Even the clowning trouble-giving monkey was a mere dot on the stage when I turned my minimising lenses in that direction. In my glare, he withdrew his fierce hatred-ridden eyes. The dangers of offending Mr. France, the imposing French teacher, had completely vanished. I dared all and cared less.

Collette and I had been so absorbed by the dancing that we were surprised when we came out of our cocooned and noticed only a handful of people left in the hall. Collette's

83

gold plated watch read ten minutes after two in the morning. We hurried out of the hall and began walking gently back to school, pregnant with love and loving. From the Moon & Star to the school campus was quite far and took a student walking normally twenty minutes to cover. As we were walking in each other's arms, and also stopping every now and then to kiss and caress, we were condemned to take more than double the time.

We arrived at a big avocado tree by the roadside, just before the path branching off to our school compound. It was renowned for tempting students with its large and tasty fruit. Collette refused to go any farther. She said we had been given the whole night off, and she didn't see what we were going back so early to do. She rejected the excuse that I had a football game at three o'clock later that day, saying that if I wanted, I could sleep in till lunchtime. So we stood under the avocado tree, wrapped in each other's arms and whispering sweet words back and forth.

All of a sudden we heard someone making their way down the little hill toward the tree. Feet arrived before us. I looked up from fashionable thick-soled Salamander shoes to find Mr. M.C. France, our French teacher, gazing at us. We were in each other's arms sharing a common pot of breathing air.

'Richard! Collette!' he called out in a threatening but tremulous voice. I alone answered. Collette simply maintained her calm as if nothing had happened to interrupt her.

'Good evening to both of you,' he said with a deliberately slow and authoritative voice and moved on, leaving us deafened by the sound of his Salamanders resounding in the quiet night air. When the man was some twenty metres away from us, Collette shouted after him with the intention of making him hear. 'Why can't that monkey leave us alone?'

'Collette, stop that!' I shouted in turn.

'I won't stop it! Why can't the monkey leave us alone?'

Thinking he was by then out of earshot, we went on whispering and caressing each other.

Instead of going ahead, he had quietly retreated to hear and see all we were saying and doing. Having done so, he issued a cough from about a stone's throw from the avocado tree, to let us know our intimate exchanges had been observed and overhead.

***

The Sunday game, a big game I approached with desire and passion, left me with a swollen knee. I was a very unfortunate goalkeeper that day. The spectators were at their supportive best and the atmosphere special. Spurred on, I was determined to keep a clean sheet, to have a faultless game. I was often surprised at how much I talked during a game. Normally of a quiet disposition, as keeper, I was a weaver bird. The rhythm of the game ran in my body. I could smell the game from a distance, like a dog of war. For the first half, my team, full of commitment and power on every break, gave me the support I needed. We had a lot of the ball, and created a lot of chances, but were only able to convert one. The injury came in the second half of the game when I went into the air to bring down a very high and fast ball. At the same time I caught the ball, an opponent who had gone into the air as well stretched out his leg to kick it. We clashed in the air, and I somersaulted and fell on my knee. My opponent was taken off the field to the Catholic Mission Hospital at Nsong, where a plaster of Paris awaited his broken leg, and where he would be taken straight home to his parents, missing out on the rest of the term.

In the meantime, I went through the last twenty-five minutes of the game without much difficulty. It wasn't until the end of the game that my knee began to swell and hurt badly. My team members carried me to my dormitory and called the college dispenser who attended to me. For three days I could not walk. The knee was badly swollen and unbearably painful. During these days Collette suffered the pains more than I. She sent me six postcards during that short time, urging me to get well quick and come back to class. All the while reports reached me that she cried everyday in the girls' dormitory. Her pain was amplified by the fact that she could not visit me in the boys' dormitory. It was forbidden for girls to visit a boys' dormitory. My friends were the closest link between Collette and me.

On Tuesday, the second full day of my injury, something happened that kept me wondering. In the afternoon, after classes were over, Mr. France, my French teacher, came into my dormitory still carrying the textbooks he had used in teaching that day. He came right over to my bed and sat by me, all full of sympathy and concern. I greeted him and he answered amicably.

'I heard in class this morning that you have not been well since Sunday. I have come to see how you are faring. I hope it is not still as serious as it was the first day you got injured.' Sympathy seemed written boldly on his face, just as it came through in his voice.

'I'm almost entirely well. I think I will try to attend class tomorrow, Sir.'

'Try and come, Richard,' he said. 'Football is a most delicate game. It needs a lot of tact and luck.' He took up his textbooks and stood up. 'I hope to see you tomorrow, Richard. Have a nice time. I am going.' And he went out without looking back.

I couldn't explain the teacher's behaviour. It puzzled me the more when I sought to understand it in the light of reason. I contented myself with the fact that people do change and that I should therefore not find it strange if the teacher had already taken upon himself to be so forgiving.

On Wednesday the teacher entered class with a face full of ropes. No student recognised him at first with all those wrinkles and a fez cap strangely perched on his head. He didn't say his usual "Bonjours, mes élèves". He ignored the whole class and sat down on the table, avoiding the chair behind it as if something poisonous had been placed on it. If Collette called him monkey then, I wouldn't have had anything against her for likening this man to an animal of low intelligence. He looked so much like a monkey that I bet with the one hundred and fifty MIM dollars still idling in my pocket that any monkey would rush to him if he went into the forest. The class must have understood that he was in no mood to be human, for they watched his ludicrous appearance with an uncommon indifference.

He asked us to take out our French books and open to a certain page. As I was still searching in my desk for mine, he rushed towards me with the speed of lightening. I heard him coming and closed my desk to see what was wrong. It was too late. Showers of slaps fell on me like hailstones on a destitute and solitary traveller in the wilderness. Bells clang-clonged in my head with mad violence, and stars twinkled in my tearful eyes.

His charge against me was that I didn't take out my textbook when he asked the whole class to do so. But he himself could see that even after his vicious attack on me about half the class still hadn't taken their books from their desks, and even those who had were yet to open their books. Every student in class exclaimed when he gave his reason for bombarding my face. They all believed there must be another reason for it. Who in class had taken out his book by the time he fell on me, beating me with the ferociousness of an enraged village drummer? He looked around and saw for himself that his reaction was embarrassingly unjustifiable.

Collette couldn't bear herself when she saw me beaten in that way. She almost stood up in outright protest but her friends stopped her in time. I could see her as she shook with rage. Her French textbook which she had already taken out and opened was put back and her desk closed. The teacher noticed it and asked her for her textbook.

'I haven't got one,' she contemptuously told him.

'Where is the one you had yesterday?' he asked.

'Missing,' Collette was still full of contempt.

The teacher knew her book was in her desk, but how could he go to force her to take it out if she didn't want to? Maybe the fear to be ridiculed more made him avoid the trap Collette had set. He left her and continued with his lesson.

On the page he had asked us to open to were a series of tough irregular verbs. He called me up and asked for the conjugation of one in the present subjective tense, which I gave. He asked for the conjugation of four more, each in a different tense, and each time I escaped the trap he was setting for me. After turning me over for long he grudgingly accepted his defeat for the day. From me he chose Collette as his next target. But with her he could go nowhere. All his efforts to make her speak were foiled. She wouldn't allow a monkey to tamper with or trample on her. When he had failed, he asked Collette to get out of his class. That was what she wanted. She banged her desk, keyed it time-wastingly and walked out in a slow snobbish manner, causing the door to make a deafening bang after her. The teacher got the frustration of his life in front of a large class like ours.

Although all this happened under the eyes of our classmates, only those who were privy to the real matter smiled with bemused understanding.

That very evening I was alone in class with Collette who was copying my notes. Our conversation dwelt much on the ridiculous and unbecoming behaviour of Mr. France. It was about five-thirty p.m. and the rest of the students were out for sports. We freely played and did things that the presence of a third person would have rendered impossible.

We caressed each other and kissed as often as the need arose. All this went on while our French teacher who had appeared out of the blue was quietly watching us through the window. I saw him before Collette did, so I told her the teacher was watching. She ignored him and intensified fondling and caressing me as if the teacher was not there. That snobbishness of Collette's must have touched him at a sensitive point of anger, for he suddenly made an about turn and walked briskly away.

The next day he succeeded in creating an excuse to suspend both of us from his classes for two weeks. We stayed away from his classes without regretting a thing. During French classes, I took Collette down to the Games Room and taught her Mathematics on the pool table. Then we discussed our relationship at length. We were, however, sure that if nothing happened to stop Mr. France from continuing to teach our class, then the two of us were doomed to do badly in the examinations. But luckily enough a report reached the Principal that Mr. France had impregnated two fat girls in town and was refusing to take them as wives. When it also filtered through that the two girls were the daughters of a God-fearing and well regarded member of the local Parish Council, the Principal had him tossed out of the college to face the charges without tarnishing the good name of the school. We were so happy about his expulsion that Collette forced me into joining her to send him a provocative farewell card.

I consider the day I made my sentiments known to Collette as the day that marked the end of my childishness and discomfort about being in the company of girls. That was in the month of May in Form Three. My three closest friends, other classmates, and even myself, had noticed the way Collette was behaving towards me.

Her behaviour was deliberately charming and coquettish. She came to my desk every now and then with simple problems in Mathematics that even a Form Two student would not have found difficult to solve. Innocently and ignorantly I solved them for her.

There was something that made me reluctant to see anything genuine or meaningful in Collette's gestures. She was an only child from very rich parents. In college she had more money per month than any of the young gentle crooks that pretended to teach us. And she was admired in our class and beyond its frontiers. How could a poor, miserable and primitive wretch of my calibre be so crazy and unrealistic as to think of declaring my sentiments to a girl of such high status: both natural and social? I was reasonable enough to know my limits.

But my associates had noticed her inclination for me and didn't relent pestering my ears with dangerous words of encouragement. If the encouragement had been from any distant classmate of mine, I would have taken it as outright mockery. But they were my friends. I knew their ways and they mine. They told me to forget about my obvious natural and social shortcomings and approach her. They claimed, and rightly too, that they were more experienced in that field, that they could read a girl's desires from her eyes and guide me in my actions. I was their complete opposite. I could be locked in a room with a girl and wouldn't know the slightest bit of what she desired except what she told me. Convinced by my friends' incessant words of encouragement, I patiently awaited the right moment. This moment was not forthcoming, because I didn't know what exactly it looked like. My friends had spoken to me of a right moment, but I had not seen any.

The moment came, however, one May day when I found Collette alone in class. I went up to her desk and greeted her but could say nothing more because my mouth would not open any farther once I had parted my lips. I tried to chase away the fear that had suddenly taken hold of me, but it had already found itself a comfortable seat. A bright idea entered my mind and I excused myself and went to my desk. She continued with her work, saying nothing. I made up my mind to write a letter to her – a letter, the exact wordings of which I have forgotten.

In the letter I told her how it was highly necessary that in an institution like ours, boys and girls should make it possible to sit and discuss common problems in an amicable atmosphere. I told her how I had read in a certain book that the student who prized his academic development above the social was doomed. And I implored her that it was imperative that the two of us should avoid such doom by developing the social aspects of our lives as well. I made her understand in very high sounding words, which unfortunately I can no longer remember, how I loved her very much. She had in fact occupied every bit of the whole volume of my heart. Which I didn't regret because I couldn't think of any other girl capable enough to deserve a bit of it, even a bit of it, I remember the particular emphasis. But I didn't forget hinting to her about my poverty. I told her how my parents were poor – toiling peasants in a remote area without a market for their produce – and how I came to school every time with almost no pocket money. I also spelt it out to her that I would be prepared to make the affair as clandestine as possible if that was what she wanted. I mean if she felt it was a gross abuse of status and position for a girl of her calibre to demean herself by going out with a boy like me. I must have ended with echoes of how I felt about her, and concluded by urging her to reply as soon as possible. My desk hadn't a lock, so I put the letter in the desk and closed it. I went to where Collette was still writing and told her I had something for her.

'What is it?' she asked, with a smile belying her surprise and curiosity.

'Look in my desk, above the books,' I told her.

'Whatever it is, why can't you give it to me?' she asked, not budging, but I pretended not to hear. So she asked again, but a different question.

'How will I like it, whatever it is you want to give to me?'

'I don't know,' I told her and hurriedly added, 'but don't forget to leave the reply at the same place.'

She looked away from me and bit her pencil.

'I am late for sports,' I told her and hurried out of the room before she could remind me that Saturday was a free day and I couldn't possibly be late for sports.

Saturday was the day the school left students free to do things of personal interest. Going to town for provisions and other necessities for the coming week was one of these things. Only the very poor like me or those who had enough to take them through the following week stayed behind on campus. Those of us who remained behind often organised football games to occupy ourselves. I was already known as a star goalkeeper, and many people were scrambling for me to play with them. At the level of the school, I had also replaced the college goalkeeper who had had a most disabling accident. So on that day when I left Collette, I went to the field and played to forget. I wanted to forget what I had just done as fast as possible. Too many scenarios were playing out in my mind. I didn't want to think of the possible responses to my boldness. What if there were no reply?

The football I played had the required effect. I forgot about what had taken place in class between Collette and me and liked the feeling of relief this brought. After the game it was about time for supper, so I hurriedly took a shower and prepared for the refectory. It was only after supper that I thought again of the letter.

I couldn't wait. I hurried to class with a pounding heart. I took the darkest paths to arrive at the block, for fear of being seen. Once in class, I plucked courage and opened my desk. A folded sheet of paper was there, lying where my letter had lain. I sighed, knowing I would know, one way or the other. I tucked the paper into my pocket and hurried back to my dormitory.

The dormitory was still full because it wasn't yet time for that Saturday evening film show. I looked around but saw no convenient place where I could read the letter without being seen or interrupted. The only place where I could freely read it alone was in the toilet. I went to my school trunk and took some toilet paper which I carried to the toilet to create the impression I was going to ease myself. I unfolded Collette's paper under the toilet light and read. It was a short letter, the words of which I remember very well. It read as follows:

'Dear Richard, I feel that what you are asking is what exists already. However, if you want me to personally give you a confirmative and formal yes, you may have it. There is something that worries me however. I would like to know why you found it so difficult speaking to me and instead you wrote. Bye. It's Collette.'

I read the letter over and over again, my heart beat growing faster with each reading. The idea came to me of going straight away to discuss my triumph with my friends. But a voice in me warned against that. So I kept the letter secret, for there was a remote fear in me that Collette could still change her mind and close on me the door she had left ajar.

That very evening she stood waiting for me at the entrance of the film hall. I didn't notice until she called.

'Richard, you haven't seen me?' She startled me with a disarmingly familiar voice.

'No, Collette, I expected to look for you in the hall.' I was already becoming a good liar.

'I thought it wiser to wait for you here, rather than send for you from your dormitory.' She was full of thoughtfulness.

93

'Let's go in. The projection is about to start.' I told her. We took a seat at the back, to avoid inquisitive stares.

I remember nothing about the film we watched, but I can never forget how I watched a film that Saturday with the very first girlfriend of my life – Collette Lansey, who was rich and beautiful, with tender reassuring eyes, and a voice that commanded as much respect as it excited desire.

Chapter Seven

When our football team played Christ the King College three days before Christmas vacation, at the field in Zintgraffstown, we lost, two goals to three. It was a tough encounter, comparable to a fight between two cocks of equal strength and stamina. We considered the final victory of the CKC boys – as they were called – an accident. They simply benefitted from their home advantage. Both teams decided the return game should be played at our college immediately after we returned from the two-week holiday.

As the captain of our team, I had to work with my teammates if we counted on winning the return game. With the Principal's permission, the college's first eleven players came back to school a week before the official reopening. We did nothing but play football, from morning to evening. I did my best to point out to my boys what was lacking. I suggested what each could do to build on his strengths and overcome his weaknesses. In the subsequent training sessions, I saw my words had not fallen on obstinate ears.

Tempting though it was, we said 'No' as a team to a suggestion by a Nsong student for us to visit a local diviner, with a good track record of making things come to pass. It was still rumoured how a previous team had done exactly that, but as it happened, the rival team had gone to see the same diviner. He told both teams that came not to score the first goal if they wanted to win the game. The outcome was the oddest game the college had ever played. Both teams would dribble to the goal mouth and suddenly fumble around and awkwardly send the ball away from the goalpost. It was only after the fact, when word went round that the teams realised what had happened. When the Principal got wind of it, he issued an injunction against 'black magic and pagan practices,' promising 'instant expulsion for those caught indulging in such superstition.'

One of the CKC players made things exceptionally difficult for me the day we played against the school. He was tall and wide and very light in complexion. He kept lingering around my goal mouth as if planted there. Though the referee whistled for offside position numerous times, he remained at my goal mouth, undeterred, spreading terror with his untrained and brutal legs. He persistently pestered me and deliberately obstructed me from going for the ball during corner kicks. This clumsy and ill intentioned boy made me think of a bull trying to use its horns to play football. Some of his teammates confided after the game that the brute knew no football but was deliberately included in the team's line up to frighten opponent players, especially the goalkeeper. I called him to tell him I would pay him back in his own rough coins at the return game. He agreed, with a glare in his eyes, to the rendezvous in two weeks time.

My preparation for the return game was two-fold. First of all I trained myself to stop every ball, no matter how tricky. I couldn't bear the thought of conceding a goal, especially with my girlfriend watching. My second target was the impressive brute. I incorporated sly techniques of playing a mean game, ones that would escape the attention of the referee. When I finally finished my personal training as well as the general training of the team, I sat down and smiled, showing my teeth, in anticipation of the triumph which awaited us.

My team as a whole was poised to attack and go beyond the limits of mere vengeance.

We told the Principal about the hospitality accorded to us at Christ the King College. He promised to do something similar in return when the CKC boys come to play at St. Martin's College, or SMC as the students called it. In my capacity as the Games Prefect, I drafted a programme for the return game, which the Principal signed without even reading it over.

Christ the King College had high academic and moral standards. Parents with the means sent their sons there, with the hope they would grow up to replace them both in position and role, and to live as responsible citizens of the land.

Girls all over yearned to have CKC boys because they were the alleged cream of the crop. The stories one heard about them were often exaggerated, but that didn't leave us boys from mixed schools unanxious each time a CKC boy was mentioned favourably.

Our school's girls were very excited when I personally announced in the refectory on Thursday that the CKC boys would be coming the next day in the afternoon, to play the return game on Sunday. Several considered this an opportunity to strike up a relationship that could mature into a promising union. Many of the Form Four and Five girls without boyfriends in the school employed new hairstyles and practiced different ways of walking and of smiling. Some girls even sought quarrels with their SMC boyfriends so as to have an excuse to do whatever they liked during the weekend. Reconciliation could come later, when the CKC boys had come and gone, not before.

Collette told me stories of how girls were infatuated with boys they hadn't yet set their eyes upon. They sat in their different dormitories, conjured up images of CKC boy and encounters with them, and let their imaginations consume them. I came to understand, from her stories, how there is much more to someone than meets the eye. The straightest looking girl can have the most fantastic fantasies.

Some of my fellow classmates spoke to me about a new girl in Form Four. They told me that the girl was, until her transfer, a student of Our Lady of the Converted Hills College, an all-girls Catholic school in faraway Zintgraffstown, our regional centre of civilisation. I wondered what could have happened to force the girl out of one school and into another in the second term. My mates told me the girl was very beautiful, but that she was equally snobbish and proud. Some of them even felt, in the hierarchies of looks they constructed, that the new girl was more beautiful than Collette. They told me how they had tried in vain to be noticed by this new girl. They complained she always talked about CKC boys – how they were handsome, urban, and well mannered. My three associates encouraged me to go to her, but I defended myself by confessing that I had not yet seen the girl, knowing inside that I was quite happy with my Collette.

The CKC delegation was headed by one of the Marist brothers who ran the school. This brother was benign in the way he went about with the arrangements for his boys. SMC students called him Brother Jesus because of his calm countenance and his long thick hair. Indeed he looked like the man imaged on the crucifix, which we had in different sizes in every room of every building, and in front of which we genuflected at mass at the start of each school day. After Reverend Brother Jesus, whose real name was Reverend Brother Goodwood, finished making every possible arrangement for the lodging and feeding of his boys, he went to Reverend Father Blackwater's house and was only seen again on Saturday morning, when he came to take his boys from St. Christopher's dormitory for a cross country race.

Among the players from CKC was a very handsome boy from the same local administrative division as me. When we played at Zintgraffstown, I had marvelled at his skill and techniques. His performance as the centre forward for his team mesmerized me. His name was Elvis Kumson

Kanson, a name hardly known beyond his village and official circles in the school. Outside the Principal's office and the classroom, his mates called him EKK, but on the football pitch he was known as KKK, to reflect the Kling Kong Kong of admirable ball reception, control, and dribble leading up to a lethal strike. Accomplished as a player, KKK was a good mover and passer of the ball and an outstanding striker in the box. He was excellent in the air and could work defensively. He was smooth, swift and precise in his game, a real master, who started strong and finished strong almost invariably. To a goalkeeper, he was like a magician playing conjurer's tricks with the ball.

Infatuated with his football, I met up with him after the game and gave him a congratulatory handshake. He was friendly. In the course of our discussion he told me how his father had died just when he was about to write his first year promotion examinations. Thanks to his good behaviour and dexterity in playing football, the Marist Brothers, full of sympathy, had taken him to stay with them and attend the college, free of charge. He also explained that after high school the Reverend Brothers expected him to get into the Marist Brothers' Training Centre in London. Presently he was a Form Five student just like me, struggling to strike a balance between God and girls, work and pleasure, learning and mischief, and winning and enjoying a football game.

EKK told me he would like to get to know a girl during their three-day stay in SMC. I promised to fetch one, but shortly afterwards, about an hour after their arrival, EKK called me off my hunt.

'Don't bother, brother,' he told me.

'What has gone wrong, brother?' I asked him in turn, wondering why he should give up all of a sudden.

At our first meeting at CKC we decided to call each other brother. When I first called him brother, I meant that he was a Marist brother in waiting. But he understood that I called him 'brother' because we were sons of the same administrative divisional soil. And so, we called each other brother, each meaning what he thought the other understood him to mean.

'Nothing's gone wrong, brother. Instead, something's gone right. I saw a girl here I knew from Our Lady of the Converted Hills College. She was with a very nice looking friend who seems to want to get to know me.

'My friend is a beauty,' he continued. 'Her father is the new senior divisional officer of Nsong. She said her father forced her to leave Converted Hills and follow him to Kibonbong. She does not seem to like this school. But I know she has her secret reasons for disliking the place.'

'What are those, brother?'

'She has a boy – Johnny Hallyday– she loves with all her heart back at CKC. I suspect it is the excessive way she misses the popstar of her heart that makes her want to go back.' He paused and looked aimlessly around my section of the dormitory. He was also the sports prefect of their school. But his rights were not as many and varied as mine; they were limited by the superimposing presence of the benign Brother who happened to love football so well.

EKK resumed, half regretting and half seeking my opinion, 'If the guy back in CKC was not such a good friend, I would have asked you to plunge into a serious campaign for the chick. But a friend is a friend, isn't it, brother?'

I cut him short by promising to show him my girlfriend. 'I have a girlfriend, brother, and popular opinion holds that she is the most beautiful girl at SMC. I will surely introduce her to you.'

'I would like to see her,' said EKK with a little sardonic smile.

'Who is this other girl you saw moving with the Converted Hills girl?' I tried to discontinue talking about Collette to avoid any rash behaviour on my part. 'She told me her name is Gladys Lamla and that she is a Form Five student.'

100

'That is a close friend of my girlfriend's. She is very unfortunate with boys. None of her boyfriends ever seems to stay with her for long,' I volunteered. Not to discourage him, I didn't add the confidence Collette had shared with me, about how Gladys had come to her in tears, a letter in hand from one of her boyfriends, with the line: "You are a very liberal fool; you want nobody to mistake you for an intelligent girl".

'But I hope to stay with her. She told me her parents live in Zintgraffstown. I could look for her at their compound. She described the location vividly.'

Our discussion became more thrilling as it took a more general dimension. We failed to notice Collette steal herself into the dormitory until she surprised both of us when she spoke. Her voice sounded so strange in a boys' dormitory. Discipline in the school that Friday evening was a little lax, and she took advantage of that to greet the special friend I told her about among the CKC players. She embraced and kissed me all over my face for some half a minute. Then she gave EKK a warm handshake.

'She is the girl I was speaking of a while ago,' I told EKK who was staring at her, his lips wide open.

'What were you saying about me, Richard?' Collette asked when EKK could not find his voice to say a thing.

'What else but that you are my baby?' I looked tenderly at her out of the corner of my goalkeeper eye.

She smiled and asked EKK, 'How is CKC?'

'Fine,' he managed to respond.

The conversation warmed up and bit by bit EKK felt more at ease. After some time Collette took leave to go to her dormitory to bring some of the 'funky' or special food she brought back from holidays. There was an assortment of what was popularly known as 'chewables': chin-chin, fried fish, beef and chicken. There were many other delicacies, the names of which I ignored, and six

101

cans of drinks. We ate and drank until the pleasure EKK felt forced him to comment after Collette went back for the last time.

'You're a wonderful guy. I must admit your appearance really deceived me at first. But now I know you're a tough guy. Tell me, brother, how did you come about that beautiful looking aristocrat?'

'The answer is simple. We fell in love with each other.'

'That is true love, brother. Nothing else can adequately explain the relationship. When you talked to me about a girl whom public opinion holds as wonderful, I thought you were kidding. Now I know every word was meant. But, brother, beautiful though she is, I'm looking at your girl with the eyes of a stranger. Maybe the superiority of your girl's beauty is but the temporary illusion characteristic of things at first sight.'

'I don't know the girl from Converted Hills, yet,' I echoed.

'You are sure to know her with time.' EKK was confident.

***

I had included a Saturday evening social in the draft programme I took to the Principal. He had signed the paper, which was a clear indication that he approved of the entire programme. But I was aware he had signed without reading. I harboured the fear that he might raise an objection when it came to the scheduled social evening. On Saturday morning I entered timidly the Principal's office to ask if the students could commence the necessary arrangements for the evening. But he didn't seem to know anything about a social evening.

'Show me the programme, Richard!' he commanded with suspicion, like a father determined to disprove his son.

I had foreseen his reaction and carried the programme along with me.

'This is it, Father,' I said, showing him the piece of paper.

He glanced over it, a shocked expression on his white wrinkled face.

'I can't believe I signed this.' He shook his head violently, so that his long hair swayed from side to side like a loose skirt dancing on a rock-and-roll singer.

His signature was clearly there on the piece of paper. No student, no matter how expert, would have succeeded in forging it. He signed like someone who had attended a special school for making signatures.

'Why didn't you explain the programme to me?' he asked in a perplexed tone.

'I thought you would ask for an explanation if you needed any, Father.' My voice was too deliberate in its innocence to be offensive.

'Do you know it entails heavy expenditure organising an evening of this nature? Eh, Richard?'

I didn't know how to answer his question. I kept quiet, a false expression of guilt perching on my face. I could say a thousand Hail Marys and Glory Bes just to show how sorry I was.

He dictated the difficult compromise at which he arrived: 'During lunch this afternoon, you should make it clear that only the Form Four and Five students are allowed to attend tonight's welcome party.'

'Yes, Father,' I said, nodding repeatedly like a gecko lizard.

But he wasn't through. 'The rest of the school should attend the normal film show in the assembly hall where there will be a roll call.'

'Yes, Father.' All I wanted was to be out of his office before he could change his mind. But he was rehearsing in his head in my presence how he was going to make sure the social did as little as possible to disrupt the normal rhythm of life on campus that Saturday evening.

'I believe the students of Form Four and Five are few enough to use the staffroom.'

Again I nodded, repeatedly, before confirming in words with, 'Yes, Father.'

'But remember to clean it up after the party. Remember to state it in clear words that only the players, if any, from the lower forms, may attend the party along with the two topmost classes.'

Satisfied with his precautions, the Principal gave me thirty thousand MIM dollars to purchase and prepare where necessary all we needed for the party.

My welcome speech at the party was said to be very interesting and rich. The CKC sports prefect in the person of EKK stood up and thanked me and the population of Form Four and Five in its entirety for the brilliant and brotherly welcome salute and reception accorded them. He ended his speech by telling me and my team that the hospitality showered on them would however not hinder his team from thrashing us the following day. My boys booed, but the girls cheered and encouraged him. In those days, if girls showed interest in football, it was for the opportunities to score goals on the social front.

The dancing started immediately after the two speeches. I was expected to open the floor formally with a girl of my choice. EKK was expected to do the same. I looked around for Collette when the record began to play and remembered she said she would be helping to prepare the food. So I went to the nearest girl I could find and took her to the floor. It was a blues number, so I held her very close to me. After the floor-opening record, she went back to her seat, leaving a rich perfume scent that sent my mind wondering what girl at SMC could afford a perfume that would leave such an aroma. Maybe she was one of the numerous Form Four girls whom I found particularly difficult to individualize.

104

EKK, on the other hand, had no time to make his choice among the lot. As soon as his name was called to join me in opening the floor, Gladys, whom he met the previous day, walked up to him. She might have sensed that any delay on her part could lead him to choose another girl just as I had done.

For six hours, the party that started at seven p.m. animated us. The music and dance was simply out of this world for students used to living behind fences like cattle. Mimboland music was blended with music from beyond – going from Boney-M to Abba through Kool and the Gang, Prince Nico Mbarga, Tim and Fotti, Nkotti François, Tala Andre Marie and Bebe Manga. The dancing was delicious and in abundance. The drinking was within measure. There was eating of food the girls prepared with some of the money from the Principal. Boys and girls freely intermingled on the floor and prayed God to double the length of the hour. I danced all the time with Collette to whom I clung like a calf to the nipple of a cow.

The football game the next day was thrilling but dangerous. The CKC brute did not forget his rendezvous with me. During the party, he had called me aside and asked if I still remembered my deal with him. I made up my mind not to forgive such arrogance. He made me remember all my sufferings during the first game. His impudence baptized my determination with fresh waters of violent vengeance.

For the first forty-five minutes of the game, we were tied at a two-two draw. Fresh coaching of my boys during half-time made them score a splendid goal within the first minute of the second half. The crowd roared wildly with encouragement for us and repudiation for the CKC boys. A group of girls and boys, probably from the lower forms, threw insulting and highly immoral words at the Christ the King College boys. They warned the players never again to set foot on the grounds of SMC to disrupt the peace and tranquillity of the students. But all their insulting words were carried away by wind to the earless eucalyptus trees that surrounded the football field.

The CKC boys were determined to live up to their pride and a sense of superiority. They made many a dangerous attempt around my goal area. I foiled all their efforts, stopping every ball that came to me. I was as aggressive around my goal as a lioness around the liar where her young ones are found. For the last ten minutes of the game, even KKK saw the tension mounting in me and abandoned his sporadic raids. Only the confident, foolish brute continued to jeer at me that the game was soon going to end without our long awaited rendezvous to match hostility with hostility. I had borne his jeers long enough. My plan was to treat him in such a way that he could, for the rest of his life, count me among the wicked men he knew.

I saw my chance, a real bright chance which I seized with competence. KKK was given a ball around my eighteen. He saw the fire in my eyes and failed to recognize me. The brute, who was playing the left wing position, shouted 'KKK' for the ball. KKK readily freed himself of the burden of making a last minute attempt to save the CKC pride. The brute rushed towards me, a mad grin on his face, ball on his feet. I timed him – a real easy prey – and somersaulting like a hydra, I landed my sharp studs on his broad chest, just when he was about to strike. He went wild with confusion and staggered for five painful seconds, his eyes wide shut. Then, as if inspired by the same supreme forces of vengeance as me, he kicked violently and wildly. I felt sharp pain on my head and knew I had been caught by the desperate kicks of the dying horse. Then he fell, and I remained grounded by the pain of his kick.

The game came to a halt as we were carried off the field, and with it our game plan to outplay, outclass and outscore our guests and rivals. It was as if some devil was hitting my skull with a huge hammer and savouring every moment of it. I touched my head where the brute had kicked and saw blood on my left hand. The last thing I heard was our Principal's voice telling Brother Jesus to drive the badly injured boy to the Catholic Mission Hospital at Nsong, on his way back to Christ the King College.

I don't remember what happened between the time I heard the Principal's voice and when I got up on Monday morning to find a portion of my head all bandaged. Reverend Sister Blueyes who taught the Form Two girls Cookery came that morning to see how I was faring. After asking whether I was making any progress, she informed me that reports from Nsong said the boy with whom I collided was in a critical state. I was still too shocked and confused to begin to regret what had happened, but Sister Blueyes being Sister Blueyes, I reluctantly yielded to her request to send the boy my best wishes for speedy recovery.

On the fourth day after the incident, I was lying on my bed looking at the four cards from Collette – one for each day since my injury – when a little Form One student who was also a member of my dormitory came rushing to my bed.

'There is a girl looking for you outside,' he told me, timidly.

'Is it not Collette? Or don't you know her?' I asked, disbelieving his ignorance. How could any boy in my dormitory not know of Collette?

'I know Collette very well, but this one is not Collette.'

'Go and tell her I'm sick and cannot come out.'

And the boy left me wondering who this girl could possibly be.

Two days after the strange girl called, I met one of Collette's friends as I tried to stroll to the refectory for supper. That was the first time I was leaving my bed since the accident at the Sunday game. The friend of Collette's I met was a very reserved girl who was hardly interested in any boy-girl affair. Her sole concern was her studies, in which, unfortunately, she wasn't doing well at all. But she was such an innately courageous girl and with high morals. She continued trying her best, despite her numerous and often near tragic poor performances. Envy wasn't and had never been one of her characteristics. She was the only Form Five student who refused to attend the party thrown to welcome the CKC boys. Just before the party that evening, she had told Collette she would not be attending because she had the last chapter of a thrilling Mills and Boon romantic novel to finish.

This girl, whom I respected as much as I did my sister Shaka, promptly accused me of double dealing when she saw me going slowly up the stairs leading to the refectory from my dormitory. I didn't understand what she meant, so I asked.

'What are you talking of, Faithful?' Her name amused me.

'I hate people who pretend, Richard. I have always considered you a good boy. Don't force me to change my mind!' She threatened me as if I would be stricken dead if she changed her mind.

'I am honestly not pretending, Faithful. I know nothing of what you are speaking.'

'What are you trying to tell me?' she was surprised. With her hands akimbo, she asked, 'Do you mean to say that that beautiful Form Four girl who has just come is telling a lie in saying that you are her boyfriend?'

I was shocked and was glad Faithful could read my countenance. For sure I was told many things about a new girl from Converted Hills Zintgraffstown, but I didn't know the girl from Eve.

'To tell the truth, I don't know the girl you are talking about, Faithful.' She could see I was sincere and serious.

'Then strange things do happen, Richard. I saw this girl telling a group of her mates that her boyfriend had been badly wounded during the football game and was lying helplessly in St. Andrew's dormitory,' Faithful narrated. 'Lucky enough, Richard, I used my authority as a dormitory captain to hush her and discontinue such a ruinous story. And lucky for you, such a story came short of reaching Collette's sensitive ears.'

I thanked her and we both went into the refectory where she trickily pointed out to me a girl sitting at a distant table. The sight of her was enough to awaken my memory from its slumber. I recognised her as the girl with whom I opened the floor at the party that preceded the football game.

Now I knew, at least from appearance, the overly spoken of girl from Converted Hills. She was very talkative and loud. I could overhear all what she was sharing, quite boastfully in the form of stories and exploits, with the other students sitting round the same meal table with her.

'You can't imagine what that man did to us,' she was telling her keen listeners. 'He stopped lectionary!'

'What!! Why?' asked one of the girls.

'He said when we dance lectionary we disturb people in church,' replied the girl from Converted Hills. 'He also wanted to stop offertory processions in church, saying that girls in procession are distracting. He said he was going to stop socials, and that if we weren't careful he was going to stop house feasts as well.'

Her listeners screamed in horror at the thought of it all.

'The Converted Hills is just like a major seminary now,' she continued, obviously delighted by the attention she was commanding.

It was only then I gathered she must be talking of the Principal of her former college.

'He says girls should tie headscarves all week long, even to study sessions and to bed. I suppose he wouldn't mind if we even wore headscarves to bathe.' She laughed, and the laughter of the others followed.

Humour certainly had a home in this girl.

'It seems they are training us to be reverend sisters. A headscarf itches when you wear it so often, but it has become a passport to go to church, or to class.'

'And what about the boys?' someone asked. 'Are they confined in similar ways?' I was able to hear the question but couldn't make out the little girl who asked it.

The girl from Converted Hills certainly liked the question, for she went on at length.

'Boys are not asked to do the same. The only thing he disturbs boys on is the belt, which must be black. The trousers as well, they have to conform to school requirements, by reducing the wide apaga width design to the pencil foot width adored by Father Lucifer.'

The girls laughed at her use of the name Lucifer to refer to the Principal of her former school. I thought it was mean of her to call him that. I didn't want to miss anything she was saying, so I divided my attention between my supper and her story. They seemed either to have finished eating or were still waiting for their own food to be served by the cooking staff of the kitchen, who went from table to table, in a refectory of 32 long tables of 10 students each. It could also be they were not interested in the fufucorn and njamanjama – my favourite – being served that evening.

'Boys have water tanks which we don't, and sometimes girls have to beg boys to carry water from their dormitories,' said the girl.

'But they should know better, since girls need water more than boys,' commented yet another girl.

'The good thing is that he enlarged the refectory. The pantry too. That's the best thing he has ever done for the school.' The girl from Converted Hills said the first positive thing about Father Lucifer.

'I bet the boys are always cheating girls,' said one of the girls. 'Our boys here always think they have to take more food than girls.'

'Exactly,' confirmed the girl from Converted Hills. 'Sometimes we have to report it.'

'Are you people at Converted Hills choosy about what you eat the way we are here?' asked one of the others.

'Ah, even more so,' said the girl. 'There girls don't drink tea; if you drink tea you are soiled. It is an embarrassment for girls to drink tea. It is worse in other schools in Zintgraffstown, where girls don't eat breakfast and boycott eating during meal times, because it is soiling to do so. When girls eat okro, they rush to brush their mouths, to give the impression they don't eat such things. Fufucorn and vegetables are soiling as well.' She laughed, and the others laughed with her.

And I understood why they weren't eating.

'Boys and girls like jeloff rice,' she went on. 'But for the rest, just like here, they have to take their own food to school – sardines, pepper, maggi, chips and other things – to substitute or supplement what they are served by the school. Another thing has come up known as poison, which girls like very much – sardines, pepper, and chips, all mixed; it is one of the top snacks at school now. When they hear you are eating poison, you are *en haut*. Cabin biscuits are not popular. There in Zintgraffstown, we are much choosier than here.'

'What other disciplinary measures were taken by Father Lucifer?' asked one of the girls.

'There are thousands!' insisted the girl from Converted Hills. 'He isn't happy if he isn't changing something to cause pain.'

The others laughed.

'You must have a Bible. The whole school, every student, has a Bible. Hymnals are compulsory at mass, and we have a French mass every Wednesday. Visiting is once a term, and there is no outing. If someone comes to see you, and Lucifer judges the mission unimportant, he doesn't send for the student, and chases the person away. Can you believe it?! Lucifer *na pepe*,' she said, drawing even more laughter.

'He cut our canteen days, limiting them to three days a week, when it used to be every day of the week. We have to wear school uniforms, no trousers. If you bring trousers, you have to pass through him, and if he says they're ok, you can wear them. Before you stage, you must ask him for permission. If you "stage", most especially girls, and are accused of distracting teachers, you are punished.'

'What is staging?' someone asked.

'Staging is dancing. You can dance as long as somebody doesn't feel distracted. Sometimes he insists you put on trousers as a girl to "stage".'

'What else?'

'You can read any type of book, but if you are caught with dirty books, they seize them. He has banned money from the dormitory. If they catch you with money, they seize it. If they steal your money, you may have the same punishment as or more than the person who stole it. They might suspend you. If you make noise in class, they may suspend you for eight days.'

'That is just like here, the noise making punishment. If we were having this conversation in class, we would all be carrying our trunks back home for ten days!' volunteered someone.

'With Father Lucifer, if you speak pidgin, you are likely to be dismissed, but you can speak Italian and German, although I'm still to find someone who does. If you are late for prayers, which we have in the morning, afternoon, and night, prayers all the time, you are punished. People are tired of prayers until they are even reciting prayers in their dreams. It is punishment. And we don't know what we did wrong. Prayer shouldn't be punishment.'

'I agree,' said one of the girls.

'There are no days of the week when we don't have mass.'

'Just like here.'

'The white Mother Superior he replaced as principal was an angel compared to Lucifer,' the girl continued. 'Only people were not seeing her qualities then. When she was there, we used to pray she should leave, but now they are praying for her to come back. We used to wear assorted dresses during her time. Lucifer's heart is hard. He beats us on the back of the hand with a gas pipe. He is very young, but he looks old because his face is always twisted with anger and bitterness. But when people see or hear him sing in public, they think he is a good man. As a punishment I once had to clear an area the size of a handball court and I cleared until I could not even hold my pen to write in class. One girl left St Gabriel College running away from Lucifer who was the Principal there at the time, only for Lucifer to be transferred to the Converted Hills she moved to. I am glad I left the school...'

Camille was her name – the girl from Converted Hills who spoke with a delightful tongue. That was what she told me when I eventually caught up with her and took her to the Games Room to fill her ears with words of how much I loved her more than anyone else. There was warmth, there were looks, there were gentle words, and before we realized, we were doing far too much for a first meeting. She was very willing to go beyond the limits of a first meeting, and I didn't see why I should force upon myself the status of a prisoner of conventions. When at last we came out of the room, we were more exhausted yet replenished than we had been when we went in. But we didn't leave the Games Room before she asked me of Collette. I told her Collette was and had been my girlfriend since Form Three, but that I did not think my love for her was still so intense. She, Camille, had most probably, and in a strikingly short space of time, stolen away the bulk of love I had for Collette. I told her I didn't regret it because the right person had stolen that love. However, I made her understand it would be greatly dangerous for her as well as for me if I abandoned Collette in a mad haste. 'It is wiser and better to do things gradually, rather than hurry matters only to bring ourselves untold complications.'

She was convinced, and for a full period of two weeks I successfully manoeuvred between the two of them without the slightest crisis. Camille longed for the day I would finally fall out with Collette to devote full attention to her. On the other hand, I had succeeded in making Collette believe that Camille was EKK's girlfriend, whom he had asked me to take exclusive care of at SMC. Thus for a while, in addition to being members of the same dormitory, Collette and Camille were very good friends. The situation was further ameliorated for me in that Camille and Collette were not in the same class; the one was in Form Four and the other, like me, in Form Five. In class I could give Collette all the comfort she wanted and spend some of my non-class time with Camille in the Games Room, all without arousing suspicion in the former.

The unfortunate day came suddenly and split my bundle of smelling shit. Collette stumbled over a highly sentimental card Camille displayed, which I sent wishing Camille a hasty recovery from a fever she had caught. In the card I wrote how I wasn't able to bear her absence any longer and wished her many sweet, lovely dreams, while promising her a box of amorous kisses. Collette sought to understand how EKK would bear that card if it was true that Camille was his girlfriend. A furious flame of anger rose in her and threatened to devour me. Instead of quenching it, her jealous friends – conspicuous among them was Gladys – added more fuel. This made her make a critical decision over a crucial and complex matter in that rash way of hers. She wrote a harsh letter denouncing me, telling me never to pass near her again and calling me a bush monkey that didn't deserve her love. That monkey word again! 'Since you are not for me, I am certainly not for you,' she concluded her letter. She added a quote I couldn't make head or tail of – 'Only a fool fixed in his folly thinks he can turn the wheel on which he sits.'

We fell out and fell apart, Collette and I. With daggers drawn, they fell out and fell apart, Camille and Collette. And the gate swung open for a new life's bargain.

Chapter Eight

Almost a week after Collette abandoned me to Camille, I was suspended from school for ten days. There was a regulation prohibiting smoking in the college. Under the influence of Camille, I was caught violating it. The Saturday that followed my falling apart from Collette was my unfortunate day with the Reverend Principal. On that day, I was smoking a stick of Benson and Hedges in the Games Room when the Principal suddenly appeared at the door. I made a desperate attempt to hide the cigarette, but he smiled a superior and disheartening smile that made me relinquish my struggle to appear holier than he. He beckoned me, with a nod of his head, to follow him to his office. There he signed a ten-day suspension paper and handed it to me, without uttering a word.

It was Camille who induced me to smoke. Without her, I never would have committed the offence of going against the regulation prohibiting smoking. I had never smoked before. Collette did not like even the scent of cigarettes. Quite unlike her, Camille would not bear a boyfriend who did not smoke. According to her, smoking, beer drinking, dancing, love, handsomeness, civilization, urbanity and modernity were compatible parts of the same body. Her intention was to mould me, with all the necessary transformations, into her dream of an ideal boyfriend.

Until I met Camille, I had always considered Collette an unsurpassable student in the field of money. Camille's coming into my life revised in a big way that conception. She was many times richer than Collette. With her, money was never a problem. Her advantage over Collette was that she came from a broken home with both parents fighting for her love. Her mother was the regional delegate of Social Welfare with residence in Sakersbeach. She hardly knew what to do with her money, having no other child but Camille. The same was true of her father who was the senior divisional officer for Nsong, where our college was located. He had not taken up another woman because he still prayed and hoped for a happy reunion with Camille's mother, whom, according to Camille, he considered wanton and recalcitrant.

Camille proudly told me how she took advantage of her parents' fight over her to interplay them, one against the other. Through her strategies, she extracted from each parent far too much money even for an extravagant girl. In matters of love as well, Camille was far more experienced than Collette. Camille was capable of turning even the most hardhearted and indifferent boy into a tender loving tool in a short time. She had already corrupted my heart with lots of money. She went as far as passing to me all responsibility over whatever sum of money she was sent. I not only stored the money but also determined how it was to be spent. Camille encouraged me to deny her money, if I judged inappropriate what she wanted it for. I was either too smart or too stupid to do that.

I showed Camille my ten-day suspension paper. Instead of showing remorse for what had happened, she jumped with joy.

'Rick! Don't you see it as an ideal opportunity for us to have a wonderful time in Zintgraffstown?'

'But you've not been suspended. I'm the one who has been sent away for ten good days! You stay right in school while I wander around like a homeless nomad!'

'Don't go mad, Rick. Wait, I have a bright idea. I can forge a letter from my mother telling the Principal to excuse me to join her in the hospital, where she is lying almost dead. Don't you see that as a bright idea, Rick?'

'Don't take the Reverend man for a little blind boy, Camille. What about your mother's signature? Do you think the Principal will accept an unsigned letter only because it comes from your mother in the mouth of death?'

'I can sign her signature without looking at what I'm doing, and you wouldn't find a single point of disparity with the original. There is also her office stamp which I stole while still a Form Two student in Converted Hills. Don't think this is the first time I'm forging a letter from my mother. I have done that many times before. I once even forged a letter from her to my father and he never discovered that the letter was not genuine. I even believe that letter to be the fundamental cause of the crumbling of their love. Not that there was much of a foundation of love to begin with.'

This girl baffled me with her words and daredevil attitude. But I was already drowning. The luxury of fear was beyond me. I would have clung even to a snake. So I resigned every effort to rise above her word. Just like Collette, Camille was not the type of girl to give up her point of view easily. I doubt if either of them had ever yielded before. Their idea of an argument was having the last word.

'What is the idea behind all this?' I asked Camille.

'I have a friend in Zintgraffstown who is a day student at Elizabeth of Paradise College. She rents two big rooms at the hospital roundabout in Zintgraffstown. She would be happy to lodge us for as long as we love to stay, for she is a friend indeed. To speak the truth, I have never met a girl who understands me as much as she does.

'But what do I do? I mean, where will I be between now and the time you successfully dupe the Principal? You know I know nobody in Kibonbong town, though I've been here for almost five years. And if the Principal catches me lingering around campus, I'm sure to be in even deeper trouble.'

'All the money is with you, isn't it?'

I nodded.

'Use some of it to secure a room at the Maryland Hilltop Hotel in town, and I will meet you there as soon as I finish with the Principal. If I don't turn up by nightfall, know things aren't going smoothly. In that case you spend the night there and wait for me in the morning.'

'What happens if you still don't turn up?'

'Don't be so pessimistic, Rich,' she reprimanded. 'You continue staying there until I turn up.'

We both laughed. Then stole a kiss and wished each other good luck. I left her still standing and disappeared from campus. The sight of the big avocado tree where Collette and I had been amorous several times and where my troubles with Mr. France intensified, gave me an awkward feeling that made me weak all over.

Camille met me at the hotel that very day, but we didn't go to look for a vehicle because she came late in the evening. We decided to spend the night there and go to Zintgraffstown the following morning. She had tricked the Reverend Father as if he was a little boy of two. It didn't even occur to the Father that he could pick up the telephone and verify from her Father who was the biggest man in town. That night at the hotel was sweet and warm, as we lay in each other's arms. I wouldn't have imagined I would feel comfortable in the company of a girl with such an expensive night gown, but I did! The inviting music of the heavy night rain on the zinc roof made us yearn more for the other, chasing sleep further and further away.

Camille's friend lived around the hospital roundabout in Zintgraffstown. She walked in a wobbly way, as if something was wrong with her hips. Maybe she had sprained them while doing some vigorous sport, or was unfortunate enough to have had an injection that led to some minor paralysis. Her name was Jerusalem, a name I found curious but cute. Camille had told me lots of stories about her, in fact, so many stories that I wondered if one person could have done all the things Camille associated with her. But, as Camille made me believe, Jerusalem had learnt to run like a teenager while still in her mother's womb.

When Jerusalem returned from church to see us waiting at her front door, happiness spread across her face. She embraced Camille more than twenty times before giving me a long awaited handshake. Camille introduced me, lining up the three names she used for me, and her friend looked me up and down and remarked that I looked handsome, 'Jesusly handsome,' she added. I was pleased to pass her litmus test, but I turned my face away when she spoke, to give the impression I wasn't interested, even if I heard the remark she made to her friend. Jerusalem unlocked the door of her house and went in with our bags, while we followed closely behind.

I looked around with incredulity at the expensive furniture, a small but unmistakably expensive refrigerator by a most comfortable looking bed with woollen blankets and pillow cases, a big gas cooker with an oven, and complex cooking utencils. Most of these things I was seeing for the first time, apart from what I had seen in books. I had missed my first opportunity to see a refrigerator in Reverend Father Blackwater's house, when I was baptized in Form One. He had asked me to come along with him to his house for a special meal, but I declined the offer because I was too shy. Back home, we consumed what we couldn't smoke or safely store away. All these things and many others were what her parlour had to show us. There was a door in the middle of one of the four walls of this room that led to the second. I remembered Camille told me right back at SMC that Jerusalem had two rooms. The wonders of this second room were as yet unrevealed.

'This is my modest hut,' Jerusalem said looking apologetically at me.

121

'It's okay.' I tried to be reserved in my appreciation. While still in the taxi from Kibonbong, Camille warned me against overly displaying approval or appreciating something, even if the thing in question was quite deserving of overwhelming praise. The reason she gave made me laugh, but didn't stop me from taking her seriously all the same. She told me that girls, particularly those with urban experience, doubted the modernity and civilisation of a boy who made such open acclamations.

Jerusalem smiled and said, 'Thank you for the compliment, Richy.' Until recently I didn't know my name was so full of versions and variants. First Camille had played with my name, and now here was Jerusalem stressing and elongating the second syllable as if saying it that way brought her great glee. Maybe these were just civilised, urban and modern ways of calling a name I had borrowed from their ranks. I was a rural village boy adopted innocently and given a Christian name when baptised as a precondition for college education. I could feel the pull of others and their ways, as they tried, each in their own way, to appropriate the child of the village that I had been until my college days, a feeling that gave added meaning to the popular saying that one is one person's child only in the womb.

'What will you drink, Richy?'

Having forgotten to brief me on what to say when asked such a question, Camille hurriedly answered for me, relieving me of my bafflement.

'He is a guy whose taste is limited to Becks and spirits,' she began, making me wonder if I or someone else was the subject of the conversation. 'His father, a very "big man" there in Nyamandem doesn't want to cheapen himself with beers poorly brewed. He is afraid of every bit of impurity that could contaminate the delicate anatomy of his favourite son.'

She laughed uneasily and fiddled with her hair. I knew she was trying to discreetly rearrange the wig on her head, one of several she wore – often along with dresses deemed too short by the college administration – each time we stepped out of the school campus. She wasn't comfortable with just being a student or simply herself.

'But you can't expect a man like Rick's father, who spent over twenty years reading and eating with whites in Europe, to behave otherwise,' Camille continued.

I didn't know what Camille was talking about. But I could see that what she said immensely interested Jerusalem, who was already revising her moderate impressions of me without the influence of my real background or actual status. This was the power and magic of the words from Camille's mouth.

Camille continued with her fairytale. 'But Rick is a little strange. He refused to study in Europe without first of all getting his Ordinary Level papers here in the country. As a prominent leader of tomorrow, he insists he wants to study in the country to get to know it thoroughly. His father, to whom Rick is the very first child, thought it better to keep him away from the booming distractions of Nyamandem city.'

As if reading that even her credulous friend might begin to doubt her, Camille added, 'Jerusalem, you see with what indifference he is sitting, as if I'm not talking about him?'

Jerusalem nodded.

'Strange guy!' Camille said in a ponderous way, and kissed my jaw with a giggle, probably meant to disguise the fact that she was taking the business of appearances a little too far.

I smiled and called her 'lovely baby.' Then I sensed the heaviness of delivering those two words, 'lovely' and 'baby', in the presence of a third party, and in particular, another girl. But I did nothing to make Camille discontinue telling fabulous lies, and I had therefore to live up to the false impressions she was diffusing, most innovatively, about me. And for nine good days! I consoled myself by thinking how brilliant Camille was at the improvisation of stories and false reasons for unexpected and often baffling situations.

Jerusalem placed a big bottle of Gordon's Gin on the central table and went out to buy the Becks which was conspicuously absent from her considerably rich stock of drinks. Camille seized the opportunity of Jerusalem's absence to caution me on many things. She also told me to say I preferred the inner room, which I hadn't seen as yet, to the outer one, because, my father trained me from when I was still a child to regard parlour sleeping as highly immoral and counter to civilised taste. Lastly, she asked me to, as if entirely of my own accord, give Jerusalem thirty thousand MIM dollars to prepare the meals for as long as we stayed with her. Jerusalem didn't stay long, but Camille had made sufficient use of the short time she was out.

Jerusalem placed the bottle of Becks on the table, and I did one of the things Camille instructed me to do.

'Jerusalem,' I called her. 'As long as I'm here, I won't have you drink anything that can be harmful to your belly.'

I tried to imitate the way our Principal talked. 'Here is some money for many more bottles of Becks. We can store them in the refrigerator for our visitors and ourselves.'

Camille looked at me with admiration.

Jerusalem took the money and went out again, her face bright with expectation.

Camille first of all congratulated me before reminding me of the next step. Jerusalem came back with a truck boy carrying four cartons of twelve Becks each. She unpacked them from the truck, and Camille assisted her in bringing them in.

Jerusalem brought two additional bottles of Becks to the table, along with three fancy drinking glasses. Once more Camille looked with absolute approval at what I was doing. I opened the bottle of gin and served Jerusalem first, then

Camille, and lastly myself. My quantity of gin was more than theirs all joined together, just as Camille had instructed in Jerusalem's absence. Then I served the Becks in the same order and finally placed each person's bottle in front of her, leaving the bottle of Gordon's Gin at the centre of the table. I took my seat again, and it was then Jerusalem's turn to say 'cheers' and wish us a hearty welcome and safe stay in her home. She did it so elegantly that my entire face shone with admiration. She noticed it and was happy.

We drank for long, but gently. From time to time Jerusalem looked across to me, and I could see nothing but admiration in her charming eyes. She didn't ask me which room I preferred but simply indicated the inner room which she thought more convenient for us. Camille got up and went into it, and came back after a minute with a smile of satisfaction on her face.

When Jerusalem and Camille were preparing supper, I called Jerusalem, just as previously rehearsed, and said, 'I think you will need a little more money for food, for the time we will be with you. Take these thirty thousand MIM dollars for now and tell me when you need more.'

She tried to thank me, but I told her not to worry, and I emphasized that she should ask for more when she needed it, knowing well enough that she wouldn't have the audacity to do so.

Once more she joined Camille over the gas cooker, and they continued to prepare the meal while I drank quietly alone.

'I hope he likes my cooking,' Jerusalem whispered.

'He is fussy, but like every guy, he loves good food when he sees it,' Camille whispered back.

'He is going to eat my food, even if I have to bring a spade and shove it down his throat,' Jerusalem swore. Then, stealing a look at me, she added, as if seeing me for the first time, 'Best Bo, your guy fine oh!! I nova see man pikin fine saute pass woman.'

125

I pretended as if I wasn't following their whispers.

Something struck Jerusalem and she exclaimed, 'Camille! Can you imagine that I didn't even ask you why you came? I forgot completely that you are students and should be in school now, busy with exams and stuff! Forgive me, Camille, I'm very forgetful.'

Camille cleared her throat in a most natural way. I was anxious to hear the latest story she had manufactured, though I didn't make known my anxiety.

'There is a retreat at SMC, Jerusalem. The non catholic students are free either to idle around the school or go for a short holiday. I thought of you and told Rick who was interested in seeing my best friend,' said Camille, with a big smile as she turned to look at me.

I smiled back at her as an indication of my appreciation of her overwhelming ability to create stories. She sounded so convincing. Here was a perfect lying machine, a veritable incubator of fables.

'Thanks a lot for having thought of me, Camille,' said Jerusalem. 'For how long are you going to be with me?'

'For nine days,' Camille told her.

'That is okay,' said Jerusalem. 'I hope you will enjoy yourself to the fullest during your own retreat.'

They both laughed and looked at me who pretended not to have heard what was just said.

'I hope so too,' Camille said, still laughing and flirting with me. They continued with the cooking, talking all the while in low tones. Sometimes they smiled at me, but I sipped my bottles of Becks, quite unperturbed.

Our stay with Jerusalem was very thrilling. She did all in her capacity to give us a nice time. Every morning before leaving for school, she prepared breakfast – dodo, pancake, puffpuff, bread, eggs and tea, or whatever was available – and brought it into our room where we were still in bed, wrapped in each other's arms and refusing to be tired of love and loving. Sometimes she returned after school to find us still in bed. But she always seemed to understand our idea of a retreat. Her friendship with Camille went back a long way.

As Camille made me understand, Jerusalem was first a student of Converted Hills, just like her, but was thrown out in class three when she was discovered to be pregnant. Being quite young at the time, she had mistaken her pregnancy for the effect of overindulging with school food. Her uncle, who was a very rich tycoon and whose main weakness was women, ironically disowned her for what he outrageously termed "her offhandedness in delicate matters." She went dejected to her home village, where she gave birth to her daughters, lovely identical twins. To continue with her studies, Jerusalem left the children with her mother in the village. She adopted the motto, "once beaten twice shy", which was displayed prominently in a well framed glass casing on the wall above her dressing mirror. This time she went to Elizabeth of Paradise College, run by the Dominican Sisters, where, with the blessings of the Mother Superior who had taken to her, she hoped to obtain her General Certificate of Education (GCE), Ordinary Level. Camille told me Jerusalem was in the same class as herself, though Jerusalem was hoping to attempt the GCE in Form Four. Camille also made me understand how there was a medical doctor working in Sakersbeach, who was interested in getting married to Jerusalem. He was the one who had equipped her house. However, Jerusalem was very reluctant to let the man know about her twin babies back home with her mother, for fear of putting him off. Her plans were to surprise the doctor with the truth after the marriage certificate had been signed. At that time, according to her thinking, the doctor would be capable of doing nothing to remedy the situation. Although himself already married, Jerusalem didn't worry about having him divorce his wife to marry her, although she sometimes wondered aloud to Camille what if, once married, another woman was to surface in the same way she had surfaced, asking the doctor to divorce Jerusalem and marry her. She was not unaware of countless examples of women fighting to death over men as lovers or husbands because they had been made to think it was *the* thing they needed the most. At a point in her life, she had even personally made herself a promise that no matter how great a guy was, even if she loved him from her ten toes to the tips of her hair, she should not fight with another woman over him. Rather wipe the tears and get on with life, as what goes around comes around. Yet, upon setting eyes on the medical doctor, her Mr. Right, her determination to marry had become too powerful to subdue. So she had convinced herself that all she needed to do was manage the facts of her life with economy, and once married, would fight tooth and nail to keep her man.

'I won't let my heart be broken twice,' she kept justifying her position.

I knew nothing about marriage and so did not attempt to advise her.

It was also during our stay with Jerusalem that I went to a nightclub for the first time. The nightclub was called Ideal World, though Camille asked me to call it IW to appear urban and modern. I called it that and nobody mistook me for the primitive bush boy that I was. If not for Camille, I would have got myself entangled in such a place. The architecture was so complex that, once inside, I found it difficult to recognise the door we used to enter the club. Colourful lights of various shapes and sizes twinkled like the stars my sister and I used to watch when we were in Safang. Giant mirrors covered the walls, and I kept walking into myself everywhere I turned. Camille was such an old face in the place that almost all the waiters and waitresses greeted her with broad smiles of familiarity and recognition. Even the imposing mirrors and mischievous lights seemed to relate to her and her outfit in a special way.

The music was good and assorted, local and international, but I could read deep disappointment on Camille's face when she realised I could not quite dance the way she had hoped.

'That is a rock-and-roll tune by Johnny Hallyday, my favourite, Rick. Let's go and dance,' she requested, leaving her seat and adjusting her wig and outfit as she looked in the mirror directly opposite where we sat.

I felt my buttocks go numb and my legs freeze at the word "rock". Camille impatiently urged me to come along. Confusion and awkwardness took hold of me, and I just stared at her in the manner of a hypnotized coward. I had never danced a rock-and-roll tune before. For a brief moment that seemed intolerably long to Camille, my mind was as inactive as a dead banana stump. When at last I regained active thought, my aim was to avoid any public disgrace. I had a capacity to bear shame as long as it was she alone who knew my shortcomings. My rapid conclusion was therefore that it would be both dangerous and foolish for me to hide the truth from her. What if I boldly made her understand I was not an excellent rock-and-roll dancer? But how would I sustain the ignominy if she asked me to come and try all the same? Hoping for the best, I rejected the temptation of half truths and told Camille the shameful truth in full, as no magic in the world could disguise my inability to dance rock-and-roll.

'I have never danced it before,' I said categorically. 'I enjoy rock-and-roll music most when I sit and watch others dance,' I told her, my face turned elsewhere. I wanted to avoid the shocked surprise on her face.

'I've never seen a guy who cannot dance rock-and-roll. What have you been doing all your life, Rick?' she asked me with a reproachful stare. 'I will dance with someone else if you can't dance,' she added in a tone of annoyance. When I just sat, she left my side and bounced down to the dancing floor.

A boy I had already remarked as the best dancer around abandoned his partner and politely implored Camille to dance. The boy looked striking in his well fitting suit of expensive woollen material. Before starting to dance, he embraced Camille with the freedom and carefreeness of an intimate acquaintance. Though that gesture shook me, I was incapable of unsticking myself from my seat and confidently walking down to the floor to toss him off my girlfriend with promise to offer better. I felt hurt by the sharp and inevitable line of demarcation and cursed Chuck Berry, the Beatles, the Beach Boys, Elvis Presley and Johnny Hallyday. On the other hand, I thanked my stars that I did not make the mistake of telling Camille a lie. She was so accomplished a dancer that, I was quite convinced, even some of those who claimed to be good dancers would decline to dance with her. The smart looking boy elegantly held and guided Camille as she made cyclonic whirls round him. Those watching them dance clapped in admiration. This hoisted the smart boy's pride and gave him the passport for more complex displays. Even though the two danced excellently and the whole watching hall expressed appreciation, I remained untouched, my hands supporting my heavy chin. It was humiliating not to be able to do with my girlfriend what she liked. Being eclipsed in the full gaze of the nightclub was not what I had bargained for when I yielded to her suggestion to go dancing – at Ideal World.

The rock music at last gave way to a blues song. I winced as the fellow pulled Camille towards him. I closed my eyes, not wanting to see what was unfolding in front of me. But God was with me at that moment that night. When I opened my eyes, I saw Camille shake herself from him and head back towards her seat, where I was mopping up streams of hot sweat from my face.

'You are a wonderful dancer, darling.' The words tumbled out of my mouth without any life in them.

'Thank you,' she answered curtly.

I was about to say something else when the boy who had just been snubbed walked up to our table. Without hesitation, he sat in an unoccupied seat next to Camille, and began speaking to her, ignoring me completely. In two gulps, I realised the gin in my glass was gone. My nerves were failing me. I shook as a village drunkard that falls into a river late in the night, on his uncertain way back home.

'Can't you see I'm with somebody?' Camille asked the intruder, a note of impatience in her voice.

'I understand,' the boy said. 'But what I can't understand is why you take up new boyfriend at SMC. How I wrong you before you leave Converted Hills?'

Camille did not answer him. She maintained her silence.

'Camille, tell me, is that why you refuse to reply the letter I send through EKK?'

That sent a bell ringing in my head. So this was the famous Johnny Hallyday, the friend EKK told me was befriending Camille when she was at Converted Hills. What an absurd coincidence! Camille caught me shaking my head understandingly.

'What is it, Rick? Have you discovered something?'

I didn't know what to say. Her question was too abrupt for an immediate answer. The urge to respond in some way forced me to say something so ridiculous that even my tensed rival was brought to laughter.

'I have just discovered that clothes appear more attractive under blue lights than under normal white light.'

'So it is because of this *great* yankee that you refuse to reply to my letter, and that you refuse just now to dance with me the blues which you often force me to dance in the past? Tell me, Camille, is this the *great* guy?' Although he didn't speak English like someone who mastered the

131

language, he succeeded in filling his condescending question with mockery and contempt. The first finger of his left hand was indignantly and accusingly pointing to my left eye, as he continued to glare at Camille without paying the slightest attention to me.

I didn't like his use of the word great, because I couldn't believe him capable of using it on me in good faith. As for the word yankee, I didn't worry myself with undue resentment because I was ignorant of what it signified.

Camille stood up, picked up her handbag, and hung it over her left shoulder. 'Let's go, Rick.'

I stood up promptly, though unsure if this was victory or defeat, and walked her out of the hall, leaving the superior dancer with his arm outreached and his finger pointing into a void. We took a taxi to Jerusalem's home at the hospital roundabout.

That night we had a lot of accounts to settle. There were a lot of reproaches and counter reproaches. Jerusalem did her best to reconcile us, drawing on the wisdom that her experience of early childbirth had brought her. Camille and I appreciated Jerusalem's efforts and retired to bed with promises to forgive and forget. But I personally learnt a great lesson from the nightclub episode. I understood how easy it was to lose a girl to an arch and more advantageous rival. That night, when Camille was soundly asleep, I got up and offered a secret prayer to God. Then I took a solemn vow to learn rock-and-roll and dance so vigorously that even my present superior rival would find himself wanting when next we met. As I fell off to sleep, I thought of my ridiculed rival and shuddered at the idea that I could have been the one abandoned like that, if things had not worked in my favour. In my dreams, I saw myself twirling a partner on the dance floor with great ease... and eventually got twirled back to village dances from my youth. I saw my maternal grandmother, an outstanding imitator. Though she had no style of her own, she was a terrific student of dancers dancing, and everyone recognised how she could outdance everyone in their style.

Back at SMC we joined the rest of the school in preparing for the examination period that was fast approaching. For me it was the mock – the examination that preceded and predicted a student's performance at the GCE in June. Camille's examination was also important. She had to pass the second term examination if she wanted to be promoted. At SMC, a student was obliged to succeed in at least two out of the three examinations to be promoted. Camille had not taken the first term examination at Converted Hills. To be eligible for class five, therefore, she was obliged to study extra hard and pass both the second and third term examinations.

We buried all sweet memories of ten days in paradise and concentrated on our studies. In the Games Room we read our books with incessant zeal. The Principal showed no sign of having carried out an investigation of Camille's forged letter. He must for sure have believed her story totally. An attitude or tendency characteristic of holy men like religious leaders, who can't imagine how some people can be outrightly deceitful. So, our lives became calm once more, and the academic atmosphere reigned supreme. My friends were satisfied and less troublesome to me. The very first day Camille and I returned to the school, I explained to them where I spent my ten-day suspension. They regretted their time wasted and cursed themselves for having worried about a clown who was busy partying with his girlfriend in Zintgraffstown.

The examination came and went. Success showed Camille and I only a phase of its bright whole. Which was very disturbing and unpleasant to me. Our mock was a tough one that kept the ink from flowing liberally out of many a student's pen. It was in fact so tormenting that teachers even congratulated students who passed three papers only, one less than the expected four in the actual exams. I however, told the school a different story as always. I was given many prizes because I succeeded excellently in all ten papers I opted to write at the GCE. The Principal relinquished his initial scepticism and gave me his full permission to do all ten papers and bring unprecedented glory to the school. It was the first time ever, in the history of the school, that such a concession was being made. No student had done ten papers before.

On the other hand, success refused to brighten Camille's face. She failed her exams. I was devastated, but not she. She gave failure such a smile of mixed triumph and mockery that I wondered for quite some time whether she was of sound mental state and responsible. Instead of expressing regret for failing her examinations, Camille was far more concerned about the seemingly distasteful fact that the long interval of examination writing had kept us away from each other.

Camille's interest was one – to drive my mind back to sumptuous thoughts of living together and falling into each other's arms. She succeeded in getting me to regurgitate the happy and sweet memories of ten days well spent, which had been blocked from our minds during the hostile examination time. In that way, she borrowed a sweetener from the past to be able to eat her bitter present.

It was the two-week Easter vacation. And June smiled mischievously around the corner. The SMC atmosphere was taut with hectic preparations for the fear-instilling GCE examination. The Principal decided that the Form Five students should stay behind while the rest of the school went home on holidays. Because classes were to proceed as usual for us our teachers were asked to stay as well. Reluctance could be read on their faces, but they were obliged to stay. Protest meant forgoing a handsome salary in a world where many barely scratched a living. And they had tasted enough of the rigour of the Catholic authorities to know the other costs of opposition.

Students on the contrary were very pleased to stay. The Reverend Father's offer, in addition to being an innovation, was a rare sacrifice at a time when many establishments were essentially into making profits. We were to be fed and lodged freely by the school. However, to ascertain the payment of our fees for the third and final term, the Father asked us to write letters to our parents or sponsors. We wrote these letters following a model he provided. He collected the letters and took them himself to the post office in Kibonbong town.

Classes started full swing the second day of the holidays. The Principal drew up a timetable in which he gave privileged positions to English, French and Mathematics. This was understandable because only a pass in all three of these subjects could guarantee a first certificate, which was what SMC needed to keep its academic flag flying.

The Reverend Father was always present. He wanted to assure himself that the school was making a worthwhile investment. Thus he saw to it that the teachers taught with a sense of mission and purpose, and that we took them seriously. We were under the guidance of the teachers in the mornings and the early hours of the afternoons, for every day of the week but Saturday and Sunday. Daily classes were to begin shortly after the six-thirty a.m. mass. Four to six every afternoon was the period reserved for sports. This was intended to keep us away from our books till seven-thirty p.m. when we again devoured them until nine-thirty p.m. That was what the Reverend Father thought good for us.

But too much zeal for success made us modify certain aspects of the programme. For instance, some students sacrificed sports entirely while others made just a once-in-a-blue moon appearance on the playgrounds. Again, at ten p.m. when we were supposed to be in bed sleeping, we students, like little Nsong children hunting for crickets, lit our hurricane lamps and went into little hide-outs. In this way we hoped to better shape our future. Reverend Father Blackwater the Principal reprimanded us time and again when he called around on night checks, or when we betrayed ourselves by dozing off instead of following the classes attentively. Despite his good intentions, he couldn't do much to stop us. With his doctrine alone, he couldn't enforce what he thought best. For instance, he couldn't sacrifice his own sleep every night to make us sleep.

We took our studies very seriously. Though very difficult, the mock GCE left more than two thirds of the class convinced they had to work extra hard. The Principal and his staff were cautious about us considering the mock as an unqualified yardstick for performance at the final examinations in June. They asked both the successful and unsuccessful not to be deluded by their individual results. None of us was to be either overly confident or too disappointed. Both attitudes were dangerous and could adversely affect the end results. We were determined to prove the mock either right or wrong. The successful worked hard to maintain or surpass their mock standards, while those with poor mock results toiled without relent, hopefully to destroy the mock's role as a reliable measuring rod. Thus for different reasons all together we toiled more than ever before.

Though pleased to see us work hard, the Father was worried. He felt we were overdoing it and could easily outdance ourselves before the real dance.

The first week passed unnoticed. Our academic activities seemed to provide time with wings, making it fly with undesired rapidity. We gave ourselves so much work that we were likely to rejoice if told the examination had been postponed to June of the next year. Maybe we also yearned for other ways of obtaining certificates than by examinations. None of us was willing to admit that it was a fear of the examination rather than a lack of time that was our problem.

On Tuesday morning of the second week, the boys were in the Physics laboratory revising major experiments with a renowned teacher the Principal had imported from a nearby high school. He was to handle us for the holidays while the authorities fished around for a qualified permanent teacher. The former Physics teacher, Mr. Newton Lawson, had abandoned his post when he obtained a government scholarship to read computer science in Britain. The specialist teacher's presence at SMC was highly appreciated. We enjoyed his professionalism and his pedagogical approach. He actually led us to believe that "the student is the teacher". We learned to find the answers ourselves. He merely roamed the laboratory observing us, asking questions, and otherwise guiding us. How could a student's dullness survive in the face of such an approach?

The girls, who were disallowed to do Physics, were in class reviewing their Cookery lessons and theorems. Reverend Sister Esther Blueyes was absent; she had gone to consult the eye specialist at the Catholic Mission Hospital at Nsong. The girls needed her supervision and guidance to revise Cookery techniques. Without her, all they could do was review their class work ...

Once, there was a timid knock at the door of the laboratory. The teacher shouted 'open' to whoever was there. It was Collette. She just opened the door a bit and slipped in like a house rat through a crevice. In her right hand was a folded piece of paper. She gave it promptly to the teacher and walked briskly out, giving the teacher no time to question her. In addition, she snubbed all the boys who, through silly noises and comments, were trying to make her feel ill at ease. My three associates were particularly naughty. They murmured and even shouted my name in a provocative manner. But luckily what they said escaped Collette's ears.

I was afraid without knowing why. Composure deserted me and fear took its place. Since we fell apart, Collette had done everything to avoid me. If I greeted her, she refused to respond. In class, she chose a seat miles away from mine. She would not bear the sound of my name from her friends. There was no dirty adjective Collette did not use on me. To her friends, she referred to me as the meanest boy in the world. Within a very short time, I had fallen from the illustrious level of the demigod of love to the abyss of a malevolent devil.

Not only was she full of hatred, she tried to poison the minds of others against me. Her brusque change of attitude made me wonder whether she was the very Collette who could have given her life for me about a year ago. She came across as someone who knew no moderation, someone as fiery in love as in hatred. How could one and the same boy be the object of such intense love and hatred from the very same girl? Are love and hatred two sides of the same coin? These were the types of questions that danced in my mind.

The teacher unfolded the conspicuous piece of paper. He read it and looked up at the class. 'Who is Richard Ngoma Lumawut?' he asked.

The whole class burst out laughing at the sound of my name. The teacher was taken aback. He thought his pronunciation of the name was perhaps faulty. So he called it again, stressing every syllable. My heart leaped. I stood up trembling.

'The Principal wants you in his office urgently.'

I stood numbly. What could Collette and the Principal be up to? I knew I had done nothing wrong. My conscience was clear! But I wasn't free from fear. The teacher asked me out so he could continue with the class. I left my books with my friends and walked out. The door was bolted behind me.

The Reverend Father was sitting in his office, a sorrowful expression on his face. He asked me to take a seat directly opposite him. On his table was an open letter. I tried in vain to keep myself composed.

'Who is Mr. Samson Samba?' the Father asked me when I sat down.

'He taught me in class seven, Father. He is a very good friend of my father. What is the matter, Father?' I was somehow relieved that Collette was not part of the show, whatever it was.

'He has written me a sad and disheartening letter. Things are not well at home, and you are being summoned home for a brief period.' The Father seemed to be deeply affected by the words he uttered. Their weight was heavy on his voice and countenance.

'What does this mean, Father?' I was very worried.

'That is all Mr. Samson Samba's letter says. He must have written it in a hurry, probably to take advantage of someone travelling from the village.'

That did not sound convincing at all. How could Mr. Samson Samba be in too much haste to inform me of what was so urgent for them to want to disrupt my studies? Just like the child that is in so much haste that he forgets to bring home the wood he set out to fetch.

The Father seemed to know my train of thought, for he hurriedly added, 'Whatever the case, Richard, I would like you to go home. But do not stay there for more than a week. I want you back within that time limit no matter how critical the situation turns out to be. Do you understand?'

My lips didn't part readily, but my head nodded.

'Here is some money. It should be enough for you to pay for transportation and for food on your way to and from Bonfuma. Take no book along. I think an extra shorts and shirt will suffice. Leave right away,' the Father told me, standing up.

139

He escorted me out of the office, adding, 'Be a man, Richard. I am proud of you. So is God.'

He turned abruptly and walked back into his office, closing the door behind him.

Chapter Nine

'Where is my mother?' I asked Lumawut's second wife, the only person I found in the compound when I arrived home following Mr. Samson Samba's letter to the Principal, summoning me.

'I am not your mother's keeper,' she retorted with shocking contempt.

'What is the matter? Have I erred? What grave wrong have I committed that you cannot afford to answer me in a less hostile manner?' I spoke to her imploringly, with deliberate politeness and calm. I avoided the urge to reply to aggression with aggression. But my diplomacy bore no dividend. My questions and presence were repugnant to her.

'Don't bother me! You better leave me alone before things get bad for you too!'

The word *too* caught my attention. It confirmed the feeling implanted in me since the Principal read out Mr. Samba's letter to me that something was wrong in Lumawut's household. My fear intensified. The fact that I did not find Mr. Samba at home and that this woman was so hostile meant I would have to rely on my own sleuth work to learn what was going on in my family.

'Where is Lumawut?' I insisted.

'Don't you dare call my husband by name again!' the woman shouted. 'He isn't your age mate!'

Something was definitely the matter. Where was Mother? Where was Lumawut himself? And my three junior siblings? And Shaka, my elder sister, who had attempted marriage and given up because her husband had failed to understand her? These questions rose and fell in me like an unfortunate

141

drunkard unable to swim out of the river into which he had fallen. There is nothing as bad as for an anxious and eager question to be unsatisfactorily answered, worst of all completely ignored.

'I have told you to disappear from here! I don't want to see you! Just continue to bother me! My husband will teach you a lesson when he returns in the morning,' she threatened.

Drawing on commonsense knowledge, I would have understood this woman's aggression if she were pregnant. But she had ceased to conceive ever since the birth of her only child and daughter. A daughter she made with her former husband and whom she adored as Christians do the crucifix. Despite what diviners in Bonfuma and beyond had told Lumawut about his wife's womb being incapable of another fruit, his love for her grew like a maize plant in the heart of the rains. He married this woman whom others hardly knew and threatened to battle it out with anyone who dared criticise his decision. And now, whatever had the two of them done to Mother!

I wasn't left in the dark for long. My little brother Newutamo and his sister Wawutalo entered the compound with large bundles of firewood on their heads. At first I didn't recognise them in their filthy rags for clothes. I studied their skinny selves in relation to the huge bundles of wood they carried. They sweated in pain, even though the sun was soft as it returned to its residence behind the western hills of Mbukan. I couldn't help but weep. But I didn't want them to see me in tears, so I turned my face away from them.

'Is that all the wood you can fetch, dogs?' the woman reproached Newutamo and Wawutalo as they put the firewood behind the kitchen. 'Fools, you eat my food for nothing! I will have to tell my husband to send you back to – whatever you call her – where she comes from.' She spat in their direction.

I watched the woman with bewilderment. I felt my eyes grow bigger and bigger.

'Fomtu, Fomtu, Fomtu...' The woman called out for her daughter.

'Mother!' A little shrill voice within the house answered.

'Come out here, dear,' she implored tenderly.

Out came the beautiful little daughter who had been tied on her back the day she strayed into Lumawut's compound like a wayfarer three years ago. The little girl's light skin made her look so different from her dark mother. She glided with the majesty of a Highlands princess, hardly letting her feet touch the ground. There were signs of disturbed sleep in her eyes. Every now and then she opened her mouth wide in an effort to yawn. Her mother held her hand in a loving way and asked her something that escaped my ears. Then in a much more audible voice, the mother told her:

'Go into the kitchen and bring out those two large calabashes. I want those useless pigs who eat for nothing in this house to go and fetch water from the stream. I hate seeing them standing idly around that foolish nuisance they call Big Brother.'

Fomtu dashed into the kitchen.

Newutamo and Wawutalo, after putting down their heavy bundles, had come over to embrace me where I was standing. The woman's derogatory remarks drowned my self control. My retaliation was prompt.

'Wherever you have kept my mother, woman, I won't stand here like a banana stump and watch you treat my juniors like kinless orphans!'

'You bark at whom?' she sneered at me. Then spat contemptuously in my direction saying, 'I have told those dirty fools to go to the stream. If you don't want the dogs to do as I say, you can carry them away from this compound. But not before you have refunded the huge sums of money my husband has spent on you ever since you went away to waste time schooling.'

143

I couldn't bear her arrogant impudence any longer. And before I could think twice she was lying on the ground, forced there by cruel blows. Ignoring her wails, tears, curses and bites, I beat her like a samba drummer would beat his dilated *kdom*. Perhaps the only difference between the way I beat the woman and the way a *Samba* drummer would beat his *kdom* is that of attitude. Unlike the latter, who beats his drum with a light clear heart, my heart was weighted with bile, which I vented through heavy blows, intended to finish her life. Not until her eyes were bloodshot, her nostrils clotted by blood, and her dark body covered with bruises did I relent. Then, with the satisfaction of a teacher who has had a headstrong pupil punished in style, I left her cursing and vomiting and crossed over into the heart of the village to visit a schoolmate and find out the whereabouts of my favourite teacher, Mr. Samson Samba.

When I came back, Lumawut was sitting on the veranda of his two-room house. I was surprised to find him because the woman had said he would not be coming home until the following morning. He glared at me. He didn't answer when I greeted him but sat on like a carved piece of wood, or a lifeless stump. His wife who was sitting by his right looked at me resentfully. In front of Mother's kitchen, that now looked like a hut where fowls went to roost, stood Newutamo and Wawutalo, their eyes fresh with tears, and their faces wearing the burden of their suffering. As I turned to comfort them, Lumawut sprang on me like a wild cat. I sank under his brutal weight. He gave me no time for self defence and made me incapable of any form of resistance. I thought I would collapse when, through some swift moves, he clasped my chest between his legs and rendered breathing difficult. As Lumawut tormented me, his wife cheered and reminded him of how I almost killed her. She came right down where we were struggling and tried to lift my feet to offer her husband an ideal chance of killing me. But our tough struggle forced her back to her seat on the veranda with wounds to lick. Lumawut muttered angrily as he bombarded me.

'How dare a bastard like you beat my wife?' He reminded me of the fact that I wasn't his son. Of course, he had known Mother was a single parent when he came seeking her hand in marriage. He had promised to take good care of Shaka and I, which he did, until this woman came along.

'Can you refund the huge sums of money I have spent on you?' he shouted, still beating. His breath rose and fell as if in greater pain than I. In beating me he tortured himself.

'Follow your evil mother back to Safang. I don't want to set my eyes on you ever again. Tell her to be ready to refund all the money I have spent educating you. Tell her to bring back my baby daughter. My wife Kang can look after my daughter, who will be safer here than with that evil mother of yours.'

He made these utterances as he beat me. When he was too tired to beat on, he dashed into my room he was once proud of and threw out my bags. Then he forced me out of the compound into the darkness of the night.

A sympathetic neighbour took me in for the night. In the morning I left my bags with the neighbour and set off for Safang. Though I couldn't recognise the road I used as a little child, I was determined to see Mother and my sisters. My anxiety made me trace the pathway despite the obstacles.

Chapter Ten

'Do not be angry, Ngoma,' Mother told me. 'What justice can you expect in a thing like this? The woman was caught red handed with my garment which she wanted to use for purposes of witchcraft. And because Lumawut loved her more, he supported her. It would have been a different story if he had not allied with her to tear me down, to humiliate me in public.' A gush of tears interrupted her. She looked for a piece of cloth and wiped her face with it. Those tears that rolled down Mother's cheeks and looked like the sacred blood of Christ pierced me like thorns and made me wild with thoughts of vengeance and justice.

'What about reporting them to the police, Mother?' I asked, desperate for justice. 'The culprits would be punished accordingly!'

'Police, what do you mean by that?' Mother expressed surprise. 'This, I must confess, is the first time I am hearing the word.' She feigned ignorance.

'They keep peace and maintain a rigorous fight to save justice from the unscrupulous and crooked in society. I have seen many of them at work in towns, especially at Zintgraffstown. They...'

'But none of these keepers of peace are here, my son,' Mother interrupted. 'They are where you have named, because people in those parts respect them. Here they would be out of place. First, because there are village councils all over our land, which are expected to perform the same functions as the police you talk about, though unfortunately these councils are far from doing their duties. The councils

147

pass judgement looking at the faces of people, instead of deciding according to the trend of the case in front of them. Second, no one in this land would find cause to respect the type of peacemakers you talk of, because they fail to have any meaning within our society.'

Mother took a detailed look round her single-room residence. There was nothing in it that could make a woman proud. She brought nothing back from Bonfuma. Lumawut didn't allow her to. She came back much poorer than she had been when we went down to live with Lumawut in Bonfuma. She shook her head and heaved a sigh of sadness. Then she spoke on, her hands spread out in resignation.

'What justice is there in this land! Lumawut and his new found love bribed them all! Corrupt beings they are, those councillors of Bonfuma!' She burst into fresh sobs.

'Can't you take the matter to the Safang council where you are better known, Mother?' I felt so angry.

'There are some of these things you don't understand, Ngoma. There are things young men should normally understand, but your somewhat soft life, devoid of the tough education our community used to give its young men, has unfortunately kept you away from the basic truths and doctrines of the land. I don't blame you for your ignorance in matters of men and power. Our complex world hasn't made things smooth for you. But those are its ways and you must learn to take them as such.'

Tears filled her eyes, and I wondered if it was possible to make ways rather than just take them as my mother suggested. I bowed my head so Mother wouldn't see the soft and teary eyed face of her boy.

'Know that our people have a saying that a cock cannot crow in a foreign land, which simply means no chief can interfere in the internal matters of another's territory without risking a conflict. If you understand this, you will perhaps know why it is impossible for the Safang council to take up a matter that is the direct concern of the Bonfuma council.

But you shouldn't worry so much about retaliation, Ngoma, for God's justice runs supreme and never fails to take its course. His may be long term, but it balances the accounts of the world. Let Lumawut and his sweetheart stay on in peace!'

'In peace?' I protested. 'Not as long as I live in this world!' I failed to get the ironic sense in which she used the word peace. 'How can they live in peace, Mother? That woman is a cheat! Why hasn't she been able to bear another child ever since she came to Bonfuma? Why do you think her first husband tossed her off, Mother?'

'Do not speak of her in that outrageous way, Ngoma. Let God judge her himself.' Mother's voice was gentle and appealing. But I was too angry to be influenced.

'And Lumawut, with a head like that of a goat! May he be struck by lightning! How can he ally with that witch to mar you, Mother?'

'I have told you to stop wishing them ill, Ngoma. God has his eyes and ears. Don't make Him think you are undermining His ability to judge for Himself. Beware!'

The sound of her voice indicated her seriousness. This time I didn't take her lightly.

I knew I would have to forget Lumawut and his wife. It wasn't an easy thing to do. As far as Mother was concerned, she had started to forget, but I came to make her wounds fresh again.

During my brief stay in Safang, I was aware of the sad moments when Mother suffered severe depression and how her once commended beauty had all but evaporated. I was deeply hurt to find Mother in this state and by the fact that I could do very little to help. As the days passed, she kept more to herself and spoke only rarely. The little baby she nursed would linger around her hopefully, but, finding no humour in Mother, would turn away and begin to cry for love and care. I did my best to make the moments less gloomy.

149

Shaka, I was told, had gone off with a Fulani herdsman who had come on a beautiful horse, promising heaven, but she was just the woman to pull him down off his high horse. Mother secretly feared for her, hoping she wouldn't end up being someone with as much facility for landing men as she had for losing them. But I was more confident, judging from how Shaka had told off her first husband who had wanted to make of her more of a beast of burden than a wife. She had walked out on him and moved on, without looking back. Even without the benefit of formal education, Shaka had given herself the option of going it alone if it came to that, while fellow females given to small battles declared victory over small trophies only to find theirs was a life of battles and despair. She was her own woman, and could bring crashing any man who came crushing.

Mother's troubles swelled unbearably with each day. She was troubled when travellers from the villages down below the mountains of Safang brought her bad news of how her children were being treated with cruelty by Kang, and how Lumawut was too involved with extra-domestic activities to supervise his wicked wife. Such stories from the mouths of strangers came to confirm what I had observed with my own eyes. All Mother heard was enough to drive her mad. But she showed extraordinary determination.

I wondered whether she wasn't trying too hard, and suggested going to the hospital, but she wouldn't hear of it. She equally declined to be taken to an indigenous medicine man, saying that the Catholic Church, of which she had recently become a member as well – thanks to the encouragement my own baptism had brought her –, was highly against any practices that predated or contradicted their gospel. The white man and his ways were zero sum games, not in dialogue and negotiation with others and their ways. Her reason for turning down the hospital was poverty, coupled with the fact that the hospital was a three-day hard trek away from our little village of Safang. All she asked of me was to promise to take the baby back to Lumawut on my way back to college, which I did. This was the clearest sign yet, that her days were numbered.

As her situation worsened, Mother turned more and more to God, to whom she prayed with all her heart. She believed firmly in His powers to perform miracles through Christ His Son. The Bible had many stories to confirm her faith. During my brief passage, I read her verses upon verses from the Bible, to prop up her morale. The evening before my departure back to college, she finally consented to see the reputed diviner of Safang, to know and deal with the real cause of her deteriorating health. I went and brought the great man to the house, and, satisfied with his promise to do everything to save Mother's life, I departed with the baby the following morning, after a long prayer session with Mother, channelled through Saint Jude, – patron saint for desperate cases. Despite her delicate and worsening situation, there wasn't the slightest doubt in me that I would find Mother alive, next time I was home. But life being what life is, that was not to be.

Chapter Eleven

For months, I was locked up in a horrible prison, painfully isolated from the bustling community outside. My powerful imagination of the outside world brought me no closer to the realities I knew so well. In that damned hell, there was no way to share my sorrows and torments. The guards were so conservative in guarding their jobs that they feared to be less beastly in looks and deeds. I was therefore with human beings who had little humanity to offer. They were strange and hostile.

My isolation became absolute. The stinking flea-infested bed made me recoil in horror. I slept on the cold bare floor, a healthier alternative, when I couldn't stand the bed anymore. It was dark all day and all night, totally dark. I guessed it was day, only when I could sleep no longer. Not that I slept much. How could I? If the guard brought me a meal, I stole a look at his wristwatch in the light of the candle he carried, to have an idea of time. The food tasted stale in my mouth, nasty and unpalatable. I needed no mirror to know how ghostlike I looked.

During the first four weeks in that prison, my thoughts centred on the GCE I had worked so hard for five years to write and pass with flying colours... on the disgrace that comes with failure... on death and dying... on...

Oh! How I felt about the GCE! Thoughts of it haunted me! How it pained me to know my mates were sitting in the auditorium, writing their way into a successful and well rounded future! I imagined them flying about with the joy and agility of angels! I saw them all great men and women, bonded together in marriage and achievement. Ready to make strong families with deep taproots, an indication of a solid, harmonious and fruitful union! I saw myself as a complete contradiction, a forlorn negation of their achievements, their class! Wearing away in a premature grave!

Yes, it is all so clear, as if happening all over again… a premature grave. Life is rapidly giving me its farewell handshake! I see the flame of my candle grow weaker and weaker with every passing second. I know my end has come. Failure, torchbearer of negation, shame of my generation, I must cede my place to God's better handiwork.

When will I stop worrying? When will these painful thoughts stop flowing? I want just a little peace of mind, just enough illusion to keep me alive for a while. Grant me a bit of peace that I may have a little rest. The thoughts are too many, O Lord. Hear my prayer! Don't you want to hear me?

The tense episodes of four weeks before have left me estranged from the world. The world I yearn to live. God has failed, despite my prayer urging him to prevent the thoughts from invading me. Again I am living the recent happenings all over! All the way back to the day all went wrong.

I see the Games Room once more. I also see Camille bending over the table tennis board and telling me what chills my entire body. I hear the Principal's words to her and see her following him out of the Games Room.

The medical doctor at the Catholic Mission Hospital at Nsong paid the college a medical visit once a term, to attend to students in the auditorium. Consultation was like a public confession of sins.

I still remember vividly his consultation with the Form Four students at that particular visit. Camille has just gone in and I am anxious and uncertain as I wait for her to come out again.

But I have the impression I am waiting too long. Will she ever come out? Sweat gushes out of my armpits, hands and face. I am worried about her. Why should she stay so long? A hopeful thought however springs up. Maybe she is planning to be examined last, to obtain a convenient opportunity to negotiate the doctor's silence on the matter. Yes, that is the idea, I convince myself. Looking at the doctor during my examination, I could see a money-minded medical practitioner in him, the sort who probably went to medical school through bribery, and since completing his training has been busy making back the millions he paid to get in. I pray the Almighty God that this is true, to help me at my hour of need.

But it happens, the dreaded. My hopes are shattered! God hasn't heard my prayer! What is He for? Just to sit up there and punish people? Who needs a punishing God? I control with difficulty a strong urge to curse Him.

I can still hear the whole of class four shouting, booing and denouncing. What must be the matter? Has a boy been discovered with dirty underwear? Or has someone peed in his shorts? My heart is beating terribly as I try to convince myself that Camille can't be the object of ridicule. But my heart is pounding wildly against my chest. Why such immense fear? I am very anxious about Camille.

Suddenly, my eyes strike a chord of reality. I see her come out. Yes, I see Camille being led out of the auditorium by the doctor. She forces a stale smile at me. What does the smile signify? A thousand years of love and steadfastness, or an eternity of blackmail, of betrayal, of shame, of remorse? She alone knows the answer.

I remain seated and watch keenly the two go up to the Administrative Block. From my position behind the entrance of the auditorium, I just need to shift a bit to follow everything going on up there. The Principal comes out of his office to meet the doctor at the courtyard. My heart sinks as I see the former shake his head with understanding, as the latter explains something. Camille is very uneasy all this while. I have nothing but immense pity for her. As I watch the scene, something happens that leaves my mouth without saliva.

Wonders will never end in this world! Evil is definitely a hundred times mightier than good. Whom do I see coming up like Collette? Yes, she is quite the one. What is she doing? She is wearing an evil smile, and waving to me in devilish fashion. Then I hear her. I hear her threaten me, saying this is her chance to teach me a bitter lesson, a chance she mustn't let go because she had prayed for this opportunity to pay me back in my own coins for what I did to her two months before. I could feel the pain in her heart and words. I felt guilty for the end of a relationship for which I wasn't entirely to blame. According to Collette, there was only one way of looking at the sad denouement. I had sacrificed her love for Camille's and had to pay for it someday, somewhere, somehow. This was her golden moment, delivered earlier than she had anticipated. But what is Collette talking about? What is it she calls her golden moment? I am confused, and the more she throws her vague threats at me the more I'm eaten by fear. What gave Collette the power to think she can act to change the course of my life? She must be mad, I conclude. But she seems determined, and laughs off my attempts to play down her threats. My attempts to play tough only make her more annoyed. She walks off, and I wonder whether I should call her bluff. But my heart sinks as she walks right into Reverend Father Blackwater's office!

What can she possibly want there? Why has it dawned on her to come for it just now? What timing! Couldn't she think of waiting a bit? Her sudden intrusion puzzles me.

Minutes later the dreaded happens. I'm dead! Reverend Father Blackwater comes out and is about to send for me from the dormitory, when he notices me sitting at the entrance of the auditorium. He asks me to follow him into his already full office. Every blessed student around the Administrative Block is looking, marvelling and questioning, but not understanding. Camille's classmates cannot give an explicit account of what made them boo and scream. Apart from that they saw Camille fidgeting in her skirt pockets, removing money, and furtively trying to offer it to the doctor. They are surrounded by crowds of students from other classes all wanting to know what happened, what is going on.

Yes, it's true that wonders will never cease. Collette has killed me. She has volunteered information to the Principal. Information that mercilessly cuts me through the spinal cord. This sorcerer of a girl tells Reverend Father Blackwater how I induced Camille to forge a letter from her parents asking him to send her home to assist her ailing mother. Collette makes the Principal understand that Camille never went to see her parents. Instead, Camille accompanied me to Zintgraffstown where we spent the ten days of my suspension from college doing things the college rules strictly prohibit any student from doing. Collette drew the Principal's attention to the fact that Camille and I left the school campus on the same day and came back at the same time ten days later. 'What a strange coincidence!' she exclaimed.

It appears to me that Collette has been inspired by the forces of evil to land me a crushing blow. The way she has taken to tearing me down greatly surprises me. And without the slightest bit of pity! Overwhelmed, I just stand and listen to her recount what she has probably rehearsed for the past several hours.

Reverend Father Blackwater is so convinced by Collette's tale, he forbids me to open my mouth. I see all his past esteem for me vanish. He outrightly denies me any chance to defend myself. How carried away by Collette's vendetta he must be! Bravo, Collette! Now I understand how one good turn deserves another. What a cruel way to make one learn his lesson!

I still hear the doctor's luxurious but flat voice. He is repeating the story of Camille's strange behaviour an hour ago, for my sake. Camille is found guilty of breaking the school regulations prohibiting fornication and pregnancy. She is declared pregnant. Reverend Father Blackwater is shocked and worried, lost in thoughts of what damage such a discovery will cause his school. Until now his school has enjoyed a very good reputation, and his pride and integrity as Principal has been great. Then this anathema! These strange pawns of the devil! They have ruined everything. What must he do to bail out the dignity of St. Martin's College? The Principal is most disturbed. He sits fuming, muttering, and cursing, and going completely red as if he will explode, then managing to regain self-control.

Finally he has a solution. It is the one way he can hope to save St. Martin from imminent disgrace. The triumphant Collette must say nothing to anyone about what transpired in the office. She has to keep the truth a secret to the outside world. The doctor must help the Principal think out an explanation convincing enough to satisfy Camille's classmates whose curiosity was rising like garri in cold water. But the truth must be buried within the four walls of Blackwater's office.

I remembered the worst of it all. The dismissal under a false pretext! Our belongings were brought to us by school cleaners, for we were henceforth considered too dangerous to come into contact with the rest of the students. We were the weed that must be picked out and destroyed, lest the year's harvest be a bad one.

When my books were brought to me from the classroom, tears clouded my eyes at the thought of a bright future so ruined. At that moment, I found myself cursing, not Collette, the Principal or any one else, but Money. Would any of this have happened were there not too much money for Camille to play around with as a student? My mind was invaded by images of money as a destructive force. I saw money at the heart of much strife in society, as a force that hindered creativity in favour of the sterile pursuit of material pleasure. Money was a machine for the production of misery and unhappiness. This plague, this pestilence, was to be avoided and shunned. 'A moneyless person is a happy person,' I told myself. 'Keep away from money if you are to remain friends with happiness,' I advised myself, as if I had a second chance.

But reality was there, anxious for its pound of flesh.

A fast telephone call brought Camille's father rushing to the Principal's office...

Chapter Twelve

'So, Elisabeth-Paradise,' I concluded, 'that's how I met your mother, the woman who abandoned you in a paper bag at the doorstep of her friend, with a note on your forehead. I am glad Jerusalem decided to take you to the only people she knew could save your life without too many questions. But I am terribly sorry your mother left you the way she did, and that I wasn't there for you. Don't be too harsh on us, I beg of you. It wasn't for want of caring...' I could hardly finish my words. I broke down in tears, and cried like never before. Getting to know at the age of forty the daughter I had fathered in my teens and should have watched and tended in her childhood years was as painful as it was fulfilling. I felt like an undeserving prodigal father.

'Father, this is not a time for regrets,' Elizabeth-Paradise reassured me. 'The important thing is that we are reunited, and that you are here for me the day it matters most in my life.'

'You are too kind, Elizabeth-Paradise, much too kind,' I felt undeserving of her forgivingness and understanding.

'I wouldn't be about to receive my final vows in my calling as a Dominican Sister, if I weren't ready to forgive and forget, would I?' she asked, looking straight into my eyes, with a reassuring calmness, that made me so proud of her. But it also made me feel so little, so sinful in her eyes. How could I say I deserved the name father, when I, instead of assuming my role and mission in life, had retreated to the village upon the first hurdle I encountered in my quest for a modern education? Was I deserving of respect as someone who had chosen to settle for little or nothing rather than fight back for his right to a dream? Why had I abandoned too easily my search to reconnect with Camille upon my release from the Juvenile Correction Institute? Why had I insisted on a job as herdsboy wandering the hills and valleys of Safang, when my favourite teacher in Bonfuma, Mr. Samson Samba, was ready and willing to recruit me as a teacher at the Government School of Bonfuma, of which he had become headmaster? Why…?

These were the thoughts that infused guilt in me, and made me terribly uncomfortable, even as I was thrilled to be in the company of Elizabeth-Paradise, following the miraculous arrival of her letter inviting me to a meeting with "the daughter you have never met." Upon receipt of the mysterious letter, something had clicked, and I had, without thinking twice, abandoned the cattle on the hills and started trekking from Safang, through Bonfuma until I arrived in Jengjeng. There I took the first lorry I saw to Zintgraffstown, where I met the daughter I had never known.

'How I wish your mother was here with us to crown this moment of your life, to seek forgiveness, and to make our reunion complete.' I sobbed like a baby, guilty for not having a more convincing answer on the whereabouts of Camille.

'God's time is the best,' Elizabeth-Paradise sought to reassure. 'Mother has not contacted me. She probably doesn't believe I am alive. But I am sure we shall reconnect one day. I can feel her in my heart. I know she is alive somewhere, and if telepathy is what I hear it is, our family reunion is just a matter of time.'

'I believe you,' I told Elizabeth-Paradise, and with those words, I felt an intimacy with her so strong that I could only liken it to what being a loving father must mean. I imagined her mother meeting her in the near or distant future, and could almost hear Camille thinking of all the things she didn't do as a mother… feeding her with the milk of life, teaching her how to cook and how to navigate and negotiate life…, and wondering what she could do to make up for everything she didn't have the opportunity of doing.

When Camille and I said farewell, we did not know it would be our very last time of setting eyes on each other. How could I have known that she would abandon our newborn baby on the doorsteps of where it all began, and vanish without trace? How would I have known that this daughter would be taken away and raised in a convent, after Camille's father, in arrogant bitterness, had declined anything to do with "a bastard baby"? How could I have imagined that his differences with Camille's mother were so deep that he couldn't even contact her to find out if she would be interested in raising her granddaughter? And that of all places, it would be the very Reverend Sisters who ran the Elizabeth of Paradise College which Jerusalem, Camille's friend in Zintgraffstown, attended that would adopt our abandoned daughter, and name her after their college, as if they knew what we knew? It was the ingenuity of Elizabeth-Paradise, her refusal to accept her truncated past, that had made possible my reunion with her, a few days before her final vows. It had taken over forty years for this to happen, but it was the greatest moment of my turbulent and disappointing life.

Now, as I sit at the Dominican Convent in Zintgraffstown, under a mango tree heavy with fruit, telling Elizabeth-Paradise stories I would have loved to share with her, if I had had the opportunity of being her father in a normal way, my mind keeps going back to that fateful day at college, some forty years ago.

I still see it with vividness, how we leave the school campus for good in Camille's father's car, after the Principal justified his daughter's expulsion. Camille was right when she told me her father is as wild as a beast. He doesn't look at me, not at all. I have the impression he has me in his car because he doesn't want to lose track of his prisoner. I'm sure he feels I'm entirely to blame in this affair. But he isn't devoid of love. Thank God. He is very mild with Camille who is sitting on the passenger seat. His language to her is not harsh at all, a remarkable contrast with his beastly roars at me. To him, I'm nothing short of a hooligan who deserves instant extermination.

Ah! Wicked thoughts! Come on if you must! Yes, I see Camille weeping bitterly as I am handed over to the forces of Law and Order. She is incapable of doing any more than shedding tears. At least she has tried and failed to make her father realise she loves and cares for his prisoner. Looking at her as I'm dragged away to prison, I feel I love her more than ever before.

I still see myself weeping in that stinking, dirty, airless cell the very first day I was brought in. How could I have fallen so low so rapidly? From images of a hero returning to rapturous welcome, to gasping for breathe like a dying rat caught in a trap set for an antelope! Thoughts of how my future has slipped away into oblivion and nothingness cast gloom over me and keep me weeping for days.

Yes, all these recollections are as vivid as if things were happening all over again and again.

A bright idea crops up. An idea that would prevent the outside world forgetting me completely. A bridging idea. Before the Law sanctions that I am a hooligan deserving immediate death, before I drive myself to death with painful thoughts, I have to write a letter to my mother, my sole parent. I want her to know the mess in which I have ended up, in the world she brought me to live. This letter, I will hide under this stinking bed. I've read how prisoners often leave messages in their cells for relatives or friends to discover. I only pray that the wild prison guard – Sergeant Wild – doesn't destroy it. I still have my pen with me. Amazingly, it stayed in my shorts pocket all along the way to this hell. There are some pieces of paper too. Thank God. No! Thank the stars these instruments are here to make it possible for me to write the letter.

Oh! I almost forgot about my unborn child! Camille will be the mother of my child in a matter of months. I'm lucky her father was afraid an abortion might cause her death. Camille will give birth to a son of mine! She can't give birth to a daughter! Girls are incapable of many things. They are traitors as well. It is a girl who betrayed me, isn't it? Camille would have kept her ground, were it not for the devilish Collette – the Vendetta who pushed me into a pot of hot peppersoup. No, it must be a son! Even the uncaring God can't dare to alter it this time! Mine is a dream quite alright, but a dream about an eventual reality. What can I do so that my son may think good of me? What can I do to prepare the kid for life?

Write a poem. A poem that can stay until my son learns to read and understand, the fate that befell me, because of jealousy, and because my poor peasant parents could pull no weight. Then Camille will give it to him as a token of goodwill from his loving father! I've done enough of English Literature to be able to compose a poem for my son. A poem which he should read when he comes of age to learn that his father lives no more.

Son, Dearest,
My mother brought me into this world
Like yours did you
One word of advice
Steer clear of womenfolk
Yet had I, you'd not be…

Then, it occurred to me. What if God, so contrary of late, makes the child a girl?

Daughter,
I suppose God has saved you from your father's fate by making you a girl

165

May the Camille in you bid farewell to your Collette
May you live the agile life, filled with achievements that
I…

'What have you learnt from life, Father, that I could use
as a compass to live my calling?' asked Elizabeth-Paradise,
in tears. She was reading her rosary with her fingers all the
time I spoke, just as was her habit every time I came to see
and share with her the story of my life, for a week now.

I reached into the innermost chamber of my soul, where
I had contemplated my being and deeds over the years.
'Make good use of the present, so as not to regret the past.
And avoid keeping for tomorrow what you can do today.
Sometimes there is no next time because of what happened
the first time,' I told her.

'It is important to keep going even in failure, for he who
fails a thousand times has discovered a thousand ways of
failing,' I added. 'Be principled, strong and firm in your
pursuit of the good and the truth,' I paused, looked at her,
and said, 'I could go on and on.'

She smiled, warmly, and took my hand saying, 'There is
much more in life than meets the eye. One person's
cleverness is like shallow water that soon dries up. Let's
join hands in prayer…'